MAGIC & MAYHEM

STARRY HOLLOW WITCHES, BOOK 4

ANNABEL CHASE

RED PALM PRESS LLC

Magic & Mayhem

Starry Hollow Witches, Book 4

By Annabel Chase

Sign up for my newsletter here http://eepurl.com/ctYNzf **and like me on** Facebook **so you can find out about new releases**.

Cover Design by Alchemy

❀ Created with Vellum

FOREWORD

You will notice that a character named Raoul makes an appearance in this book. Don't be concerned, you haven't missed a chapter in a previous book. His introduction can be found in the short story anthology, *Seven Pets for Seven Witches*, which will be released in January 2018.

Furthermore, please note that no gnomes were harmed in the writing of this book.

CHAPTER 1

FLORIAN and I zoomed toward Balefire Beach in my silver sports car, the aptly named Sylvia. Usually, I'd say my cousin was the quintessential bachelor playboy with more money than sense, but since he was the reason I was behind the wheel of this sleek beauty, the least I could do was refrain from insulting him…for the next five minutes.

"This sand sculpture competition is a great idea, Florian," I said. "Your sister must be happy with you." Aster Rose-Muldoon served as the head of the tourism board and Florian had recently decided to join the team in an effort to please the family.

Florian smirked. "For once. Mother is thrilled as well. Anything I do that justifies her footing the bill for my new boat is a win for all of us."

Hyacinth Rose-Muldoon, Florian's mother and my aunt, was widely regarded as the toughest witch in Starry Hollow, except when it came to her only son. Florian's father died ten years ago and Aunt Hyacinth seemed to overcompensate by spoiling the only remaining wizard in the Rose-Muldoon family. With his white-blond hair, extreme good looks, and elite magical heritage, he was used to being spoiled by the world at large.

Florian instructed me to bypass the parking lot and pull the car straight onto the sand like we owned the whole beach. A typical Rose-Muldoon move.

"Do you think this is a good idea?" I asked, hesitant to leave the car.

Florian glanced at me, perplexed. "Five seconds ago, you said it was a great idea, Ember. You've suddenly changed your mind?"

I shook my head. "I don't mean the competition. I mean this brazen park job."

Florian looked around as though noticing our location for the first time. "What? I always park here, lazybones. If we park any closer to the water, we may as well have taken the boat."

Give me strength. "Let's go, Florian. I want to check out these sand sculptures before the tide comes in." I was covering the competition as a fledgling reporter for *Vox Populi*, the weekly paper owned by my family. I had no journalism experience, whatsoever, when I arrived in town, but my aunt decided that was no impediment. She wanted me to have a job, so now I had one.

"You don't need to worry about the tide," Florian said. "There's a magical barrier in place to protect the sculptures from being washed away by the water." He tapped the side of his head. "I believe I've thought of everything. I'm more than a pretty face, you know."

I couldn't wait to see what the paranormals of Starry Hollow came up with for sand sculptures. I'd seen quite a few competitions back in New Jersey when I was a kid, and I still remembered how talented some of the sculptors were. Images of Bruce Springsteen and Mount Rushmore, so detailed and intricate from tiny grains of sand. Humans found a way to make art from pretty much anything.

I struggled to keep up with Florian's long, graceful strides. He made me feel like a drunken cow in a field of prancing unicorns.

"So? What do you think?" Florian asked.

"I have never in my life seen anything quite like it," I said. I was shocked that I'd managed to form any words at all. And here I thought Bruce Springsteen and Mount Rushmore had been impressive. The Balefire Beach competition put sand sculptures in the human world to shame.

"Once in a while, I pull a frog out of the cauldron," he said.

I scratched my head. "That doesn't sound like a good thing."

He blinked at me. "You wouldn't want a frog in your stew, would you?"

"As a general rule, no." I focused on the first sculpture on the beach since it was impossible to miss. "Sweet baby Elvis. It's an actual castle."

Florian grinned. "It sure is. Looks like we can even go inside. Come on."

The sandcastle took up roughly fifteen hundred square feet of beach. It had arched doorways and windows, spires, a tower, and a flag waving proudly at the top.

"Who did this?" I asked.

"I did." A pixie fluttered beside us. Her hair was streaked with orange and yellow so bright, the colors reminded me of a sunrise. "Maisie Cranshaw, pleased to meet you."

"You sculpted this all by yourself, Maisie?" I asked in utter disbelief. I couldn't even make a castle out of Lego bricks. My fine motor skills were highly questionable.

"My wings make a big difference," Maisie said. "They help me with the higher parts of the structure."

The height was only one of many reasons to be impressed. "You must use pixie dust," I said.

"A pinch here and there, yes," she said. "That's to be expected. The only participants that make sand sculptures without magic are the ones that don't have any."

Magic or no magic, the castle was unbelievable. When Maisie offered a guided tour, Florian and I jumped at the chance. The interior was even more detailed than the outside, if that was possible. There was a full dining room with chairs and a long table, all made from sand. Florian sat at the head of the table and tapped his nails. "Where is my bucksberry fizz, Simon?" He pretended to ring an invisible bell, one of his mother's habits. "And bring me my Precious. My lap is far too cold."

I bit back a smile. No way was I going to join in the ridicule of Aunt Hyacinth. I wouldn't put it past her to cast a spell where her ears burned whenever someone dared to mock her so she could exact magical revenge.

"Maisie, this place is incredible," I said. "Is this your first competition?"

"Yes," she replied. "I've made sandcastles here for fun before, but never as part of a competition, and never on such a large scale. I decided to go all out for this one because of the prize. The Magic Words has a fantastic supply of history books, but they're very expensive. The gift card is ideal."

"Can we actually go up the spiral staircase?" I asked.

She nodded. "It supports up to three paranormals at the same time." She giggled. "I was tempted to follow the building code just for fun, but it is a castle, after all. Hard to follow the same rules."

I took the spiral stairs up to the second floor and peered out the window. The entire stretch of beach beyond the castle was filled with sand sculptures. I couldn't believe the turnout. This was definitely going to become an annual event. I bet it would draw tourists from other paranormal towns in future years. We'd need to have Aster include it in the next brochure.

"We're going to be here all day," I said. "There are dozens more out there to see."

"I see a mermaid I'd like to have a closer look at," Florian said.

I surveyed the beach for the mermaid sand sculpture. "Where? I don't see it."

Florian pointed. "Not 'it.' Her. Over there, climbing out of the surf."

I groaned. He meant an actual mermaid. I watched as she toweled off her fin and transformed them into human legs. Neat trick.

"You go hit on the mermaid," I said. "I want to check out those other sand sculptures. I'll need to bring Marley back after school. She'll go nuts." In typical Marley fashion, she'd probably want to join the competition. The prospect made me cringe. My magic was too elementary to compete in this landscape. I wouldn't want to disappoint her. Maybe next year when she came into her own magic, she could participate.

I admired the sculpted chamber pot and other medieval accessories before returning to the beach.

"Thank you so much for letting us take a tour," I said. "I wouldn't be the least bit surprised if you win."

The pixie's cheeks were tinged with pink. "That's kind of you to say, but you haven't seen any of the others yet."

"I don't need to," I said. "I'd like to take a few pictures for the paper, if that's okay." I took out my phone and tapped on the image of the camera.

The pixie appeared pleased. "I would love that. My students will think I'm famous."

My brow lifted. "You're a teacher?"

"Yes, I teach history at the high school. If I'm not teaching history, I'm usually at the library reading about it. History is my passion."

"Do you teach paranormal history only? Or do you include human history as well?" I asked.

"Mostly paranormal, but it's hard to avoid human history as it has impacted us greatly over the years," she replied. "I've always been fascinated by castles, though. The medieval period is my favorite."

"Your students will be jealous that you took the day off to play on the beach," I joked.

"We're very fortunate to have days allocated to pursue personal projects," the pixie said. "I know in the human world people tend to be limited by sick days and vacation days. We have those, but we also have passion project days, which are great for events like this one."

What a brilliant idea. "Isn't that great, Florian?" I turned around, but my cousin was gone. I spotted him walking along the beach with the mysterious mermaid. Leave it to Florian to find a date in any situation.

I continued wandering down the beach, marveling at the sculptures. The next one I came across was a giant coffin. I had to admit, it was a bit disappointing after the castle, but the attention to detail was amazing.

"Go on," a voice urged. "Lift the lid."

My head jerked toward the source of the sound. "There's not something scary in there, right?" I didn't do scary very well. I refused to watch any horror films or tour haunted houses. Those kinds of thrills didn't appeal to me.

The vampire gave me a patient smile. "I promise nothing will bite you. A vampire can't promise much more than that."

Gently, I raised the lid and peered inside the coffin. My eyes widened. "It's you." He'd sculpted his own image in the sand. "This is so cool." The image inside the coffin was an exact replica of the vampire that created it. Every detail was perfect, from his thick eyebrows to his Roman nose.

"I'm so glad you like it," the vampire said. "The name's Thomas, by the way. Thomas Enders."

"It's nice to meet you, Thomas. I'm Ember Rose. I work for *Vox Populi* and I'm writing a story about the competition."

His expression brightened. "I'm glad it's getting so much attention. It's good to have activities that bring the town together. There's often so much that tears us apart."

"I wholeheartedly agree." Even though I was still new to Starry Hollow, I liked the tight-knit community far more than the sprawling suburbia back in New Jersey. "What inspired you to do this?"

Thomas glanced down at the coffin. "I quite like the idea of capturing a part of yourself that you can never see. Like seeing how you look when you close your eyes. I wanted to sculpt what I look like in my sleep."

"Well, you did an amazing job. It's an exact likeness."

He clasped his hands together. "Thank you so much. I don't have the magic that some others have, so it's nice to know my hard work is appreciated."

"Good luck in the competition," I said, and continued down the beach.

The next sculpture appeared to be a maze. I stood at the entrance, debating whether to venture in.

"Don't worry. If you get lost, I'll help you out. Just don't let the minotaur in there get you first."

I whirled around to see a middle-aged man standing beside me. His brown hair was receding and a few faint wrinkles were noticeable around his eyes and mouth.

"Is there really a minotaur in there?" I asked. I didn't put anything past these enterprising paranormals.

He chuckled. "Not a real one. Only made of sand, like everything else you see here today. I encourage you to seek him out, though. He took me longer than the maze, but he's worth it."

"Then I have to find him, because this maze is awesome," I said. "How long did this whole thing take you?"

He looked thoughtful. "I was so immersed in my work, I lost track of time."

I had no doubt. Sculpting hundreds of thousands of grains of sand was worse than herding cats, in my opinion. Not that I had any experience in herding cats. To date, I was strictly a dog owner.

"If you like, I can hand you this spool of thread," he said, opening his palm to reveal a ball of bright blue thread. "I used it when I was working to make sure I could find my own way out."

"That was very clever of you," I said. I took the spool and put it in my pocket. "If it starts to get tricky, I'll whip this out."

"Or I can simply escort you," a familiar voice said. "Miss Rose is known for getting herself into trouble now and again. What kind of gentleman would I be if I failed to assist her?"

I smiled at my editor-in-chief, the smoldering vampire, Alec Hale. "What are you doing here? I thought we agreed the competition was mine to cover."

"And so it is," he said. "But everywhere I went this morning, residents were raving about the results, so I decided to see for myself." He motioned to the rest of the beach. "It is every bit as inspiring as they claimed."

I gave the sculptor a knowing look. "This is one for the history books. You've managed to impress the most unimpressible vampire in Starry Hollow."

Alec gestured me forward. "After you, Miss Rose."

As I entered the maze, my stomach became a whirling dervish at the thought of Alec being close to me in such restricted quarters. There were several instances where the path narrowed and we had no choice but to brush against each other.

"A maze was an interesting choice," Alec said. He placed a guiding hand on the small of my back and my spine tingled. "In the middle of a busy beach, yet it still feels secluded."

"It sure does."

The maze twisted and turned until we found the minotaur in the middle. The sculpture was a full head higher than the sand-based hedges around it, even though I couldn't see the head from outside the maze. The horns were long and curved and the face resembled a bull more than a man.

"He's oddly attractive," I said, fixated on the massive chest.

Alec coughed a laugh, an unusual noise from the typically refined vampire. "I suppose I can see the allure. There's a reason why *Beauty and the Beast* has become a classic."

"I didn't expect the competition to be such a success," I admitted. "I thought there'd be a few sandcastles as high as my waist and some pet sculptures. Maybe a Sphinx."

Alec's green eyes glimmered. "And now you're in awe of our hidden talents."

"No hidden talent there," I said, and touched the minotaur's bicep. It was as firm as it looked. "It's all pretty obvious."

"Yes," he said, his gaze pinned on me. "It really is."

I swallowed hard, acutely aware of the fangs protruding from the sides of his mouth. I knew what that meant now, thanks to a few well-meaning residents. If I'd had fangs, mine would've been dragging along the floor of the maze right now, covered in sand.

"You need to do a better job of cloaking your thoughts, Miss Rose," Alec warned.

I squeezed my eyes closed, mortified that he heard what I

was thinking. "Or you could simply choose not to eavesdrop."

"We're in a confined space," he said. "Our senses are heightened. I could no sooner avoid your thoughts than you could avoid having them."

"I thought we agreed not to acknowledge any...special thoughts," I said. Our attraction was impossible to ignore, but we both knew it made no sense to pursue it. For starters, he had deep emotional issues thanks to some fairy who played him for a fool years ago. He was also my vampire boss, and my aunt was ridiculously selective about the men admitted to the family. No matter how much she liked Alec, he would never be a wizard and, thus, never good enough for me.

"We're not acknowledging anything right now," Alec said.

"Except this minotaur's amazing backside," I exclaimed, breaking free of Alec and working my way around the sculpture. "You could bounce a sand dollar off it."

"What an...interesting suggestion," Alec replied. "Something you would do in the human world?"

I cleared my throat. "Nope. Not me."

Alec gazed at me with affection. "I rather like this maze. It's as though we've been transported to another world where it's only the two of us."

I gestured to the minotaur. "Technically, it's the three of us."

Voices over the hedge suggested others were working their way to the center of the maze. "Ah, it appears our isolation is short-lived. We should make haste."

I tried to hide my disappointment. "Come on, Alec. Time to find our back to reality."

CHAPTER 2

MARLEY WAS every bit as excited as I expected to see the sand sculptures after school. I took her through the castle and watched her marvel at every detail, including some I'd missed the first time.

"A two-headed axe," she exclaimed, lightly touching the sand axe affixed to the wall of the castle. "The sculptor is so talented."

"She's a teacher over at the high school," I said. "Maybe she'll teach you history when you get there."

"Not if I attend the Black Cloak Academy," Marley replied.

"Don't get your hopes up," I advised. "We don't know for certain that your magic will manifest next year. You need to be patient." Not a virtue for either one of us, sadly.

"It will," Marley insisted. "I can feel it." She closed her eyes as though to emphasize the point. "I'll come into my magic at eleven, just like I'm supposed to."

"There's no 'supposed to,'" I said firmly. "Your father was a human, so there's no guarantee. And, remember, I didn't come into my magic until this year."

"That's only because of your dad," Marley countered. "If he hadn't done a suppression spell on you, you'd have known you were a witch years ago. Our ancestor is the One True Witch. That means our magic is super strong."

I had no desire to get into an argument about a past I couldn't change. "The sun is starting to set," I said. "We should hurry before it gets too dark to see the rest."

We exited the castle and I demonstrated the maze to Marley. It was much easier now that I knew the correct twists and turns. I tried to block out the image of Alec's elegant body moving alongside mine as we explored the perfectly formed paths.

"This minotaur is awesome," Marley said, admiring the structure. She jumped up to try to touch the giant horns on his head, but she was too short to reach.

"I'd lift you up, but you know I'd throw my back out," I said. My lower back was the bane of my existence. I could sneeze wrong and end up in bed for two days.

Marley cocked her head. "Why don't you use magic? You have your wand, don't you?"

I frowned. "I don't know any spells that would give you a boost. I'm still a beginner, remember?" I hadn't even scratched the surface of my magic powers yet. My aunt was determined that I be a star pupil, though, and had set me up with various tutors to hurry the process along. I had no doubt that she viewed my abilities as a reflection on her and was trying to avoid embarrassment.

"Think of all the basic spells you've done so far," Marley said. "I'm sure you can modify one of them for this purpose."

"For this purpose?" I repeated. "One of these days, Marley Rose, you're going to sound like a child. Promise me that."

She gave me a broad smile. "When I'm ninety and suffering from dementia, then I promise."

I crossed my arms. "If you're ninety, that means I'll be…" I didn't dare say the word. Marley was far too anxious for me to mention the possibility of my death, even as a joke. Having lost her father at a young age, she tended to be clingier than most kids her age. I had to admit, though, since we arrived in Starry Hollow, she'd loosened up quite a bit. It was a welcome change.

Marley studied the height of the minotaur. "You know what? I'm having flashbacks of McDonald's when you had to rescue me from the top of the slide because it was too high."

I didn't miss the toddler days one single bit. "Good point. Should we leave it then?"

"Yes," Marley replied. "I don't know what I was thinking."

"To be honest, I'm glad you considered it, if only for a moment," I said. "It's good to test your boundaries. Break out of your comfort zone."

"Says the woman who will only wear one brand of lipstick," Marley said with a roll of her eyes.

"What? I'm a loyal customer," I objected.

We found our way out of the maze and Marley pointed to the sand sculpture of the coffin. "We missed that one."

"Okay, fine," I said. "But that's the last one tonight. These sculptures aren't going anywhere for two weeks. We can come back and see the rest another time."

She skipped ahead to the coffin and touched the exterior that was crafted to resemble wood grain. "I don't know how they do this. It looks so real."

"I know. You can lift the lid," I told her. "It won't be as cool because the vampire who made it isn't here, but you'll still get a kick out of it."

Marley recoiled. "Nothing will pop out at me, will it?"

I fought the urge to laugh. Like mother, like daughter, apparently.

"No, no," I reassured her. "Thomas made the sand sculpture inside the coffin a likeness of himself. That's all it is."

Marley placed a hesitant hand on the lid and slowly lifted. She peeked inside and smiled. "He has a very pleasant face, although his nose is a bit funny."

"What's funny about his nose?" From what I remembered, it was Roman rather than weird.

"I think he's had a nose job," Marley giggled.

I peered over her shoulder to get a better view. She was right. The sculpture seemed to be falling apart. The eyebrows were now blended with the rest of the head and the nose was smashed. Even the body looked more like a cocoon than the detailed vampires cloak from earlier.

"I wonder if Thomas has seen this," I said. "Maybe he can fix it before the official judging begins."

At that moment, a gust of wind blew past us, kicking up sand in all directions. The loose sand on the vampire scattered and I gasped in horror.

"Marley, look away," I snapped.

"Why? What's wrong? Did his cloak blow open?"

If only. I pulled my phone from my pocket. "I need to call the sheriff."

"Because someone tried to sabotage the vampire's sculpture?" Marley asked. "It isn't really a job for the sheriff, is it?"

I stared into the coffin. "Maybe not...but murder certainly is."

Sheriff Nash swaggered across the sand, looking out of place on the beach in his tight jeans, plaid shirt, and boots. Deputy Bolan was behind him, struggling to keep pace with the werewolf's longer legs. The leprechaun scowled when he saw me.

"It always has to be you, doesn't it?" the little green deputy asked.

"It's not like I seek it out," I said. "Marley and I were enjoying the sculptures when we found the body."

Sheriff Nash surveyed the area. "Where's Marley now?"

"I asked Florian to come pick her up," I said. "She's anxious enough. I didn't want her to see any more than she had to."

"This is certainly going to put a damper on Florian's big tourist idea," Sheriff Nash mused. "Nice to know that not everything he touches turns to gold. Makes the rest of us mortals feel better about ourselves."

I squinted at him. "Shouldn't you be more concerned with the dead body in the coffin than whether Florian is getting knocked down a peg?" The sheriff's prejudice against my family was fairly relentless. He'd made it clear to me on multiple occasions that he disapproved of my family's position of power in the community. In his view, my aunt was a *de facto* leader in Starry Hollow and he resented her influence.

The sheriff studied the outside of the coffin. "I'd like to look for clues before we destroy it."

"Do you have to destroy it?" I asked. "Thomas worked so hard on it. It seems a shame."

Sheriff Nash cast a sidelong glance at me. "If you can think of a way of getting the body out without sacrificing the sculpture, feel free to speak up now, but I don't have time to wait for one of your coven members to get here with a magical plan."

I was still too green to conjure the right spell. "Go ahead, I guess."

"Now don't go sulking, Rose," the sheriff said. "You've been a witch for five minutes. You can't expect to know everything."

Deputy Bolan took out his phone and began taking

pictures of the crime scene. "This won't take long. Then we can excavate the body."

Sheriff Nash looked at me with amusement. "I would've loved to see the look on your face when you realized what was actually inside the coffin."

I made a face. "This whole incident just fills you with pleasure, doesn't it?" I said.

He gave me a lopsided grin. "Don't be like that. You know I like to give you a hard time."

I folded my arms. "Yes, I'm familiar with your certain brand of charm."

He chuckled. "Any idea who's in there?"

"A young man," I said. "That's the extent of my identification skills. I didn't recognize him. No horns or wings that I could see. Honestly, I was more concerned with shielding Marley."

The sheriff nodded. "Because you're one of those broomstick mothers."

"I haven't even started broomstick lessons yet," I shot back.

Behind me, Deputy Bolan strangled a laugh.

I fixed him with a menacing stare. "What's so funny?"

"That's not what a broomstick mother means," the leprechaun replied.

"Well, I certainly don't beat her with one," I said hotly. Although I wouldn't mind knocking both of these guys over the head with one right now.

"It means you hover," Sheriff Nash said, one eye trained on the crime scene. "You need to give her more freedom. Let her experience life a little."

My jaw tightened. "What do you suggest? That I let her see a few more dead bodies at the tender age of ten? That's your recommendation? No wonder you and Wyatt are so screwed up."

He took my barb in stride. "Admit it, you're a broomstick mama," he teased. "I'm gonna get you a T-shirt to wear so everyone knows the truth."

"Go ahead and see where that T-shirt ends up," I said. Marley called this particular tone of voice 'getting my Jersey on.'

"All done here," Deputy Bolan said. "How do you want to remove the sand?"

"The old-fashioned way," the sheriff said. He and his deputy began scraping away the sand.

"He's got pointy ears," Deputy Bolan said. "I don't recognize him, but I'm going out on a limb and say an elf."

"We'll have to try to ID him," the sheriff said. "Contact transport, Bolan."

Deputy Bolan shot off a text.

"You sure you didn't see anyone out here earlier?" the sheriff asked.

I shook my head. "It was starting to get dark, so Marley and I were finishing up. There wasn't anyone else around. The coffin was our last stop before we planned to head home."

"And you said the vampire that created this sculpture is called Thomas?" Sheriff Nash typed notes on his phone as he spoke to me.

"That's right," I said. "Thomas Enders."

"I know the name. Enders runs a funeral home in town," Deputy Bolan said.

"I guess that explains the coffin," the sheriff said.

I frowned. "I thought being a vampire explained the coffin." I sighed. "He was really nice and so proud of his work. He's going to be crushed when he sees this."

"He'll be more disappointed to learn he's part of a murder investigation," the sheriff replied.

I put my hands on my hips. "I highly doubt Thomas is involved in this. He would never want to ruin his creation."

"You don't know how long the body has been here. Maybe Thomas chose this sculpture in order to hide the body."

"He runs a funeral home," I said tartly. "I would think he'd have easier methods."

The sheriff shrugged. "Paranormals do desperate things in times of need."

"Like that time we were on a stakeout and you drank too much water," the deputy said. "You had to shift into wolf form and then peed on the fire hydrant." The deputy began to laugh at the memory, but stopped abruptly when the sheriff failed to join in.

"Well, I was covering the competition for the newspaper," I said, "but it looks like I'll be covering a murder instead." Poor Florian. One of his good deeds was finally going to get recognition, but it would be buried by a true crime event. "Will you call me when you ID him?"

Sheriff Nash gave me a cocky grin. "I'll do you one better. When I find out his name, I'll take you out to dinner and tell you all about it."

I groaned. "Are you sure you want to keep doing this?" I asked. "We could just leave it at the mild flirtation stage and call it a day."

He winked at me. "Now, Rose, where's the fun in that?"

CHAPTER 3

Hazel swept into the cottage, lugging the Big Book of Scribbles. Technically, the book was filled with runes, but to my stubbornly untrained eye, the markings appeared to be nothing more than a toddler's handiwork.

"You're going to throw your back out carrying that book around all the time," I said.

The Mistress-of-Runecraft set the book in front of me and opened to a new section. "My back is as strong as a Kraken's, I'll have you know."

I gave her a curious look. "Seriously? How'd you manage that? Because mine is as strong as an arthritic ninety-year-old's. It doesn't seem fair."

"Stop trying to divert me from the lesson," Hazel said. She tapped the book with her wand. "There are more runes than minutes in the day, so we have a lot of ground to cover."

I groaned. "I rue the day I was introduced to runes."

"That's not remotely funny," Hazel said. "However, if you applied yourself to runes with the same gusto, you might actually learn something."

"Doubtful," I said. "The only things I like about ancient

Egypt are the pyramids and the cat gods." I held up a finger. "Oh, and that Cleopatra was a badass."

Hazel sucked in an irritated breath. "How many times must I remind you that runes are not the same as hieroglyphics?"

I shrugged with mock innocence. "As many times as it takes?"

Hazel slammed the book closed, nearly catching my fingers in the process. "I am well aware that runecraft is not your favorite subject, Ember, but let's not waste each other's time."

I pushed back my chair. "Couldn't agree more. I'll walk you out."

Hazel's wand shot out like a streak of lightning. "Not so fast." She murmured an incantation under her breath and my body went rigid.

"Are you kidding me?" I couldn't move a muscle, except my mouth. It was like she'd tied me to the chair with invisible duct tape.

"Maybe next time you'll be more cooperative," Hazel said.

"Ha! If you think I'll learn my lesson, then you don't know me very well."

Hazel squinted at me. "That's not something you should be proud of. Now, on to the lesson. My soap opera's on at lunchtime and I'm not missing today's episode. The evil twin is finally going to meet her sister in an epic showdown."

I laughed. "Hazel, if that's how you're spending your time, you need a boyfriend."

"Says the witch who sleeps with her daughter," Hazel shot back.

"Hey! That's not my choice, and Marley has gotten a lot better lately." It was true. Marley used to insist on sleeping with me every night back in New Jersey. Her arms and legs moved like the hands of a clock, giving me countless bumps and bruises over the years. My injuries had been greatly reduced since we moved to Starry Hollow.

"I'd like you to interpret these runes," Hazel said, trying to redirect my attention to the newly opened page.

"You're the Mistress-of-Runecraft," I said. "Shouldn't you be able to interpret them yourself?"

She narrowed her eyes. "I should've included your mouth in that spell."

"But then I still win," I said triumphantly. "I get to do nothing."

"I'll tell you what," Hazel said. "I'll undo the spell if you promise to get through this one page with me today."

"Where's the incentive?" I asked. "If I can pass the time sitting here immobile, that's not so bad."

She flicked her wand at the chair, which began to bounce. "Had your usual cup of tea this morning, did you?"

It didn't take long to figure out what she was up to. "Ugh. You win, Hazel." Everyone knew I had the bladder of a nine-month pregnant woman.

Hazel folded her arms and waited, a mischievous gleam in her eye. The crazed clown was playing hardball with my bladder. I didn't stand a chance.

"Okay, okay," I said, more urgently. "I promise to finish the page."

"Today," Hazel emphasized.

"Yes, yes. During the allotted lesson time. Now let me go!" My muscles burst free of the spell and I bolted for the bathroom.

From behind the bathroom door, I heard Hazel's muffled laughter. "I do love being a witch sometimes."

I washed my hands and yanked open the bathroom door. "I'm a witch, too, remember? You won't like it once I learn some of these spells and turn the tables on you." I gesticulated wildly. "The grasshopper will become the master."

Hazel blinked. "I have no earthly idea what that means."

"Me neither," I said. "But I've seen enough martial arts movies to know there's a kid called a grasshopper and the old dude that teaches him is the master."

Hazel stiffened. "So I'm the old dude in this scenario?"

"What? It means you're very wise." I sailed past her and resumed my place at the table.

Hazel pointed to the first line of runes at the top of the page. "Can you tell me what these mean?"

"Only if you can tell me when I'll ever use runes in everyday life," I replied. "Do I need them to pay bills? Grocery shop?"

"It's not geometry," Hazel said hotly. "Runecraft can be useful in coven life."

"Name one way."

She eyed me. "If I give you an advanced lesson, will you promise to keep it to yourself?"

"I thought my aunt wanted me to be advanced."

"She does, but at the right pace." Hazel twiddled her thumbs. "This is probably a mistake."

"Then you have to show me," I said. "I'm an expert when it comes to mistakes."

"Fine," Hazel huffed. She reached into her cloak pocket and retrieved a few items that looked like Scrabble tiles.

"Let me guess. A high stakes game of Scrabble is in your future and you're hedging your bets?" I asked. "Which letters do you have there? A 'q' and a 'u'?"

Hazel glared at me. "They're carved with runes." She held her palm open and I studied the shapes on the tiles. "I can use them for spells in a pinch, if I need to."

"If you drop your wand down a crack in the sidewalk?"

"Or I'm disarmed," Hazel said. "I have runes as a backup."

A knock at the door startled us both. I glanced over at PP3 snoring soundly on the sofa. Some watchdog.

"Don't your friends know your schedule?" Hazel huffed. "Oh wait. You don't have any friends."

I opened the door. "Hey, Sheriff."

"It's called a phone, Sheriff," Hazel said. "No need to drop in, especially when we're in the middle of an important lesson."

I squinted at Hazel. "You and I have different definitions of 'important.'"

"We've identified the elf," the sheriff said, ignoring Hazel. "I'm heading over to talk to the family if you want to join me."

"What happened to dinner?" It didn't have to be dinner. I would've done a full night of howling at the moon with the werewolf pack if it meant getting out of runecraft.

"Another time." The sheriff looked glum. "He was just a kid, Rose. Grover Maitland. Seventeen. A local high school student."

Oh no.

"Is this about the body in the coffin sand sculpture?" Hazel queried. She seemed to realize what we were discussing.

I nodded. "Marley and I were the ones who found him."

Hazel recoiled. "I didn't know that. How awful."

"My aunt will want me to cover the murder for the paper," I said. "We need to keep the rumors from getting out of hand so it doesn't spoil the competition."

Hazel clucked her tongue. "Florian finally gets to do something worthwhile and it ends in tragedy. Go figure."

"I hope this doesn't put him off," I said. "I haven't seen him this engaged in a project since I met him."

"That's because you haven't seen him at Elixir with three fairies right before last call," the sheriff said.

I arched an eyebrow. "Trying to decide which one to bring home?"

The sheriff snorted. "No, trying to decide how to fit all three sets of wings inside his tiny sports car."

Ah. No one could accuse my cousin of being an under-achiever when it came to his romantic life.

I turned to Hazel. "Sorry, but duty calls."

"And what about my duty as your teacher?" she demanded.

"Dead elf trumps Scrabble tiles," I said. "It says so right in the Big Book of Scribbles."

Hazel shook a finger at me. "Your next lesson will be twice as long to make up for this."

I smiled. "I look forward to it."

"You can thank me later," the sheriff whispered, and escorted me out the door.

"Do you think it's possible someone tried to sabotage the competition to get back at Florian?" I asked, as we drove across town to the Maitlands' house.

The sheriff gave me a sharp look. "Get back at Florian for what?"

"I don't know. For being perfect?"

He rolled his eyes. "I won't rule anything out. Not until we have more information."

We pulled into the driveway of a modest two-story house. The front garden was well cared for, as evidenced by a variety of flowers and shrubs. An apple tree stood sentry on the side of the house. The red fruit was so bright on the branches that I was tempted to go and pick one.

"Now, let me do the talking," Sheriff Nash advised. "This won't be pleasant."

"Of course," I said absently. I was so distracted by the apples, that I veered off the walkway and tripped over a ceramic garden gnome, kicking it down the path. "Ouch!"

The sheriff turned around. "Rose?"

"I'm okay." Although my big toe throbbed, the gnome got the raw end of the deal. Ceramic pieces scattered across the pavement. "Crap on a stick." We were about to deliver devastating news. The last thing the family needed was a minotaur like me in their emotional china shop.

"Can't take you anywhere, Rose," the sheriff said, shaking his head. He bent down and collected the pieces. "It should be easy enough to glue back together. They'll have more on their minds than a broken piece of pottery."

I snatched the pieces from him. "These are tiny pieces. It'll never be the same."

The front door opened and an older elf's head poked out. "Thank goodness, Sheriff. I guess you got our message about our son. He still hasn't come home. We're worried sick."

The sheriff straightened. "As a matter of fact, I have news about your son, Mrs. Maitland. May we come in?"

Mrs. Maitland noticed the fragments in my hands and frowned. "Is that Jimmy?"

Sweet baby gnome. The pottery had a name. My stomach turned. They lost their son and now they lost Jimmy, their beloved garden gnome, thanks to my clumsiness.

"I'm so sorry, Mrs. Maitland," said. "I was so in awe of your apple tree that I didn't see the gnome. I tripped over him and he broke. I can glue him back together, or maybe there's a spell someone could do…" I'd have to ask my cousins.

Mrs. Maitland continued to stare at broken Jimmy. "Grover gave that to me for Mother's Day." Her eyes welled with tears.

And now it would be the last present she ever received from him. I was beginning to regret accompanying the sheriff and I was sure he felt the same.

"Everything all right out here, Dottie?" Her husband

appeared behind her in the doorway. His expression shifted when he saw the sheriff. "Thank the gods. Any news, Sheriff?"

"Maybe I should go," I mumbled.

"Too late, Rose," Sheriff Nash said quietly. "You're here now. May as well make the best of it."

We retreated into the house where Mrs. Maitland brought me a small bag to hold the pieces of Jimmy.

"I'm truly sorry about this," I said. "I'll do whatever you want. I'll see if someone can magic it back together."

"Please have a seat," Mr. Maitland said. He gestured to the living room, where the sheriff and I squished together on a small floral sofa. "Can I get you anything? We still have some tea biscuits that Dottie made at the weekend. I've got some ale or lime fizz."

Sheriff Nash waved them off. "We're good, thanks. I need to talk to you about your son."

Instinctively, Mrs. Maitland reached for her husband's hand. "Go on, Sheriff."

"I'm sorry to tell you this, but his body was discovered on Balefire Beach, buried in one of the sand sculptures." The sheriff made a noise at the back of his throat. "In the coffin."

Mrs. Maitland cried out and buried her face in her husband's arm. Mr. Maitland gaped at us, shock coloring his narrow face.

"I don't understand," Mr. Maitland stammered. "How?"

"We don't know yet," the sheriff said. "We've only just identified him."

Mrs. Maitland wiped the tears from her eyes. "Is there any chance he accidentally buried himself? I've heard horrible tales of children burying themselves in the sand for fun and then suffocating." She closed her eyes and shuddered. "Is it possible that's what happened to Grover?"

"It's one possibility," the sheriff admitted. "But it would

have been nearly impossible for him to cover himself with sand and attempt to re-create the vampire sculpture over top of him. Someone else had to be responsible for that. If he wasn't alone, then that suggests murder."

"Or, at the very least, criminal negligence," I said.

The sheriff shot me a look of surprise.

"What?" I said. "I sit next to Bentley in the office. He never shuts up."

Mrs. Maitland brightened momentarily at the mention of Bentley's name. "You know Bentley?"

I nodded. "We work together as reporters at *Vox Populi*." Bentley was an elf and the brother I never wanted. We quickly developed a sibling rivalry at the office, competing for stories and vying for Alec's attention.

"Bentley used to live on this block," Mr. Maitland said. "His parents moved when he left for college."

Mrs. Maitland squeezed her husband's arm. "Grover was so young then."

"Was Grover the type of elf that would have buried himself for fun and then expected his friends to dig him out?" the sheriff asked.

"They play practical jokes on each other," Mr. Maitland said. "Steal each other's garden gnomes, that sort of thing. Nothing ever got out of hand. They're good kids."

I glanced at the bag at my feet. "Not this garden gnome?"

"As a matter fact, it was," Mr. Maitland said. "They each bought one for their mothers for Mother's Day. Later on, they went around kidnapping each other's and taking pictures of them in odd places. It was hilarious."

A single tear streamed down Mrs. Maitland's cheek and she didn't bother to wipe this one away. "It's one of the reasons I'm so fond of Jimmy. It reminds me of such fun times. Grover is…was a great joy to us."

The front door swung open and a young elf came in, no

older than twelve, dragging a backpack on the floor behind her.

"Cindy, I told you before to pick up your backpack when you walk," Mr. Maitland said. "This is our daughter, Cindy."

Cindy studied us with interest. "Are you here about my brother? Do you know what happened to him? He didn't come home last night."

"That's what we're trying to find out," I said. Cindy was only about two years older than Marley and I felt immediately protective of her.

"Cindy, we have some terrible news," her father said.

"We should get out of your way," the sheriff said, rising to his feet. I followed his lead. "I'll be in touch. Please contact me if you think of anything, anything at all."

Cindy stared at us and I knew tonight was going to be a difficult night in the Maitland household. I didn't want to witness a young girl's life changing forever. I'd already been through it myself and then again with Marley. Those experiences were more than enough. If I ever saw Cindy again, I'd recognize her by the haunted look in her round eyes.

Once we were outside, the sheriff touched the bag in my hand. "Take the gnome to your aunt. If anyone can fix it, she can."

"I feel awful," I said. "Those apples were blinding, though. Did you see them?" I had a whole new appreciation for Snow White's willingness to eat the apple brought by the ugly, old witch. I mean, I'd always thought it showed a certain level of stupidity on her part, but now I totally understood.

As we drove toward Rose Cottage, the sheriff kept a firm grip on the wheel, careful not to make eye contact with me. "I hate this part of the job," he finally said. "I think I'll head to the Wishing Well. Any interest in joining me in lieu of dinner?"

I got the distinct impression that he didn't want to be

alone. Since Marley was already set up for the evening with our household brownie, Mrs. Babcock, I had no legitimate reason to refuse.

"Sure," I said. "Only one drink for me, though. I've got a busy day tomorrow."

The sheriff managed a smirk. "If there's one thing I've learned about you, Rose, it's that one drink is never enough."

CHAPTER 4

HALF AN HOUR LATER, we sat at the bar in the Wishing Well.

"You make me sound like an alcoholic," I complained.

Sheriff Nash gestured to the half-empty cocktail in front of me. "How many is that again? Refresh my memory."

I pulled the drink closer to me, shielding it from his view. "It's only number two."

"Which is more than one, the number of drinks you claimed you'd have." The sheriff signaled to the bartender for another ale. "I'm not judging you, Rose. I just think you should have better self-awareness."

"I'm self-aware," I said indignantly. I was self-aware enough to recognize the werewolf was sitting dangerously close to me. I jerked my knee away so it was no longer touching his.

"The Maitlands should be drinking with us," Sheriff Nash said. "They need it more than we do." He buried his scruffy face in his hands. "I can't imagine what they're going through."

My fingers gripped my cocktail glass. "I can." Marley and I were no strangers to loss.

He gave me his full attention and I caught the look of mortification that flashed in his brown eyes. "Great Goddess of the Moon, I'm sorry, Rose. Of course you can."

"It wasn't murder, though, and it's certainly not the same as losing a child," I said softly. The mere whiff of potentially losing Marley was enough to send me into cardiac arrest. "But loss is loss."

He dragged a hand through his thick, dark hair. "Your parents and a husband. Don't underplay it, Rose. That's definitely up there."

I polished off my second drink and slid the empty glass toward the bartender. "They won't ever get over it, but they'll find a way to keep going. Eventually."

When the bartender went to refill my glass, the sheriff motioned for him to stop. "She's only drinking to keep me company. I think she'd like a water now."

I stiffened on my stool. "Don't speak for me, Granger Nash." I smiled at the bartender. "One more, please."

"It's Sheriff Granger Nash to you," the werewolf growled. "Another ale for me."

"Well, well, well. What do we have here?" Wyatt Nash sauntered toward the bar. I'd been so focused on the sheriff, I hadn't seen his brother come in. "How do you think Hyacinth Rose-Muldoon would react to seeing the two of you so cozy?"

"We're not cozy," I said. "We're commiserating."

"Tough day," the sheriff added, and took a sip of his fresh ale.

Wyatt plopped into the stool beside his brother. "I'll have what he's having. Put it on his tab."

Sheriff Nash grunted in response.

"Is this about the dead body in the sand coffin?" Wyatt asked.

The sheriff groaned. "You heard already?"

"Damn straight," Wyatt said. "That Thomas dude was devastated about his sculpture. Apparently, he's down there now, trying to recreate for the competition."

"Didn't Deputy Bolan close off the area as a crime scene?" I asked.

"I think he was too busy being annoyed by you to remember." Sheriff Nash heaved a sigh and passed his full ale to his brother. "No rest for the weary."

Wyatt winked. "Pretty sure it's no rest for the wicked, but I'll take care of your drink either way."

"Are you sure you want to head over there now?" I asked.

"If Thomas is involved, then now is our best bet to get something out of him. Besides, he's tampering with a crime scene." The sheriff tossed money onto the counter and slid off the stool. "I can drop you home on the way."

I tipped back the rest of my cocktail. "And let you grill poor Thomas after a few ales? Not a chance." I paused, contemplating the 'few ales.' "Do you want me to drive?"

The sheriff laughed. "Werewolf metabolism, Rose. I'm fine. Comfortably numb, but fine."

I didn't think comfortably numb was such a good thing, but I kept it to myself. Instead, I followed him back to his car. We sped back to Balefire Beach and found Thomas alone on the beach, wearing a headlamp.

"Nifty headgear you've got there," Sheriff Nash said. "Did you wear that last night, too, when you buried Grover Maitland?"

Thomas frowned. "I wasn't here last night. I usually reserve use of the headlamp for midnight in my garden of good and evil." He waited for a beat. "That was a joke."

"Oh," I said, and forced a laugh. "I'm sorry about your sculpture, Thomas. I know how hard you worked on it."

The vampire glanced at his coffin. "I'm more upset about the body you found inside. There are dozens of sculptures out here. They could've used any one of them. Why did they choose mine?"

"Do you think you were deliberately targeted?" I asked.

Thomas tapped his index finger on his chin. "I don't see why. It just seems like a lot of work when the killer could've simply tossed the body into the castle or dragged it into the maze."

"Maybe they were trying to buy time," the sheriff said. "Hiding the body in your coffin meant that it might have stayed hidden for a full two weeks. Enough time for the killer to cover his or her tracks."

Thomas smoothed a section of sand on the coffin. "Because the competition ends in two weeks?"

"That's right," the sheriff said. "The killer knew this and chose your coffin because it was the best place to hide the body in plain sight."

Thomas placed his hands flat on the coffin. "I wanted to create art and instead I created a nightmare for a family."

The sheriff's expression turned grim. "Only if you killed him."

"Naturally, I didn't kill him," the vampire snapped. "I didn't even know him."

"Not all murderers know their victims," the sheriff said. "That's a fact."

Thomas took a careful step back from the coffin. "It's also a fact that I had nothing to do with this murder," Thomas said. "I bury paranormals for a living. I know the grief it inspires." He shook his head. "I'd never willingly inflict that pain on anyone."

Sheriff Nash studied the vampire for another moment before grunting. "We'll be in touch, Enders. Don't make any plans to leave town."

I shot Thomas a sympathetic look as I hustled after the

sheriff. It wasn't easy to run on sand, but I did my best to keep up with him.

He drove slowly down the long driveway that led to Rose Cottage. Other than the car's headlights, the only visible light was from the twinkling stars above.

"I'm sorry if you thought I was hard on him," Sheriff Nash said. "But I can't go easy on a suspect just because you think he's a perfectly nice vampire after spending ten minutes with him."

I was torn. On the one hand, I understood. On the other hand, I wanted him to trust my judgment. I had good instincts, whether he wanted to acknowledge them or not.

"I get it, Sheriff," I said. "Thanks for the drinks." I left the car and headed up the stone walkway to the cottage. I was surprised when I heard hurried footsteps behind me.

"Rose," he said.

I turned around so quickly, I walked straight into his chest. He caught me in his arms, but instead of pulling back, he pulled me closer. Before I knew it, his lips were locked on mine. He tasted like a mixture of salt and ale. I felt unexpectedly comfortable in his embrace. When our lips finally parted, I couldn't hide my disappointment.

Sheriff Nash grinned when he saw my reaction. "Just one, Rose. You've got a busy day tomorrow, remember?"

Although I knew it was the cocktails talking, I didn't care. I grabbed him by his shirt and pulled him toward me. "If there's one thing you've learned about me, Sheriff, it's that one is never enough."

Marley smoothed the front of her blue dress. "This is so pretty. It was really nice of Miss Haverford to send this to me." Artemis Haverford was an elderly witch and the town matchmaker. She lived in a beautiful old house with her familiar and her ghostly manservant, Jefferson. Marley and I had befriended her not long after we moved to town and had made it our mission to give Haverford House and its owner matching makeovers.

I laughed. "I think she was secretly worried you wouldn't have an appropriate outfit to wear to tea. Whatever the reason, it was a nice gesture. The color matches your eyes."

We loaded PP3's pet carrier into the car and headed to Haverford House. This was the dog's first visit and I wasn't sure how he'd behave with the cat, but Artemis had insisted he come along. If the visit didn't go well, we'd leave him home next time.

"Someone else is here," Marley said, pointing to a car in the driveway.

At that moment, the front door opened and a genie floated out. "He must be a client," I said.

Marley squinted. "How does he hit the brakes if he doesn't have any legs?"

As if on cue, the genie floated closer to the ground and human legs appeared. With a friendly nod to us, he walked to the car and got behind the wheel.

Marley and I exchanged amazed looks. It was still so easy to be wowed by what we witnessed in Starry Hollow. I may have been jaded in New Jersey, but there was no such thing in this paranormal town.

I retrieved the carrier and Marley and I went to the front door, where it immediately opened.

"Thanks, Jefferson," I said. Although I couldn't see any sign of him, I knew the apparitional manservant was responsible for letting us in.

"Hi, Jefferson," Marley said, waving to the empty space. "This is our dog, Prescott Peabody III."

PP3 barked a greeting.

"Where's Artemis?" I asked.

"In here," an elderly voice croaked.

I opened the carrier and scooped PP3 into my arms. I decided to hold him until he became acclimated to the new environment.

"What are those?" Marley asked, as we entered the old-fashioned parlor room. I glanced at the coffee table where a bunch of tiles were scattered.

"They have runes on them," I replied. "Hazel showed me some like that during our last lesson."

Artemis's lips drew back to reveal yellowed teeth. Clearly, it was going to take more than one round of whitening to brighten and lighten those chompers.

"That's right," Artemis said. "I was casting runes for my client. We ran a bit off schedule. I'm terribly sorry."

I sat on the loveseat in front of the table and set PP3 beside me. "You were using magic for matchmaking?"

"Not really," Artemis said. "Runes have many uses. For me, they were acting more as an oracle."

I flipped over a few of the tiles and studied the markings. "So they're like Magic 8 Balls. You ask a question and the runes answer?"

"I don't know what an eight ball is, but I suppose that's the gist of it," Artemis said.

"What did the genie want to know?" Marley asked. "Did you tell him his future?"

Artemis tapped her long, curved fingernails on the table. That witch's nails grew like weeds. I'd asked Jefferson to clip them only a week ago!

"I told him one possible future," Artemis replied. "Nothing is set in stone."

Marley kneeled in front of the coffee table and touched a rune. "You don't believe in fate?"

"There's nothing to believe," Artemis said. "Fate is a

fictional concept. The future is ever-changing, depending on the decisions you make."

Marley frowned. "What's the point in asking then? If you tell him the runes say he'll meet the love of his life tonight, that could change between now and then, depending on the decisions he makes."

Artemis cackled softly. "A fine mind, this one has."

I rolled my eyes. "Tell me about it. Fine enough to induce a headache when the questions start pouring in."

Artemis crooked a bony finger at Marley. "Your questions are always welcome here, young lady. Inquisitive minds are in short supply these days."

Marley's eyes shone with pride. "So is he going to meet the love of his life soon? Is that what the runes told you?"

"I can't reveal confidential information," Artemis said. "But I can demonstrate." She cast a sidelong glance at me. "Why don't you think of a question you'd like answered, Ember?"

I faltered. "About my future?" I waved her off. "That's okay. I'm good, thanks."

"Do I detect fear in your voice?" Artemis clucked her tongue. "And you pretend to be so tough."

I straightened in my seat. "I *am* tough."

Artemis gathered the tiles and placed them in a small brown bag. Then she handed the bag to me. "Gently shake the bag and, as you do, think of the question you'd like answered."

Reluctantly, I took the bag and shook it.

"Be sure to stick to a single question or the universe will get confused," Artemis cautioned.

"Have you seen the state of the world lately?" I said. "I'm pretty sure the universe is already confused." I tried to decide on a question. "It has to be about my love life? Can't I ask whether I'm going to have pizza for dinner?"

"The universe is not interested in such petty matters," Artemis replied.

"I would think in the grand scheme of things, my love life is fairly petty, too," I said.

"Love is a connective force in the universe," Artemis said. "It should never be underestimated."

I focused on my question. "Okay, I'm ready."

"Choose nine tiles from the bag and hold them in your hand for a moment. Be sure to focus on your question," Artemis instructed.

I chose nine tiles and rubbed them between my hands, keeping my eyes closed for good measure. "Now what?"

"Scatter them on the coffee table."

I did as I was told and opened my eyes. Some of the tiles were facedown and I moved to turn them over.

"No, no," Artemis interjected. "Leave them be. The ones facing up in the middle of the table reflect your current situation. Let's consider those first."

I examined the markings closely but had no idea how to interpret them. Unsurprisingly, Hazel would be very disappointed in me.

"Multiple suitors," Artemis said, tracing the runes with her finger. "Well done, Ember."

My cheeks felt flushed. "I don't have multiple suitors."

"Sure you do," Marley said. "Sheriff Nash obviously likes you. And so does Alec."

"But they're not *suitors*," I objected. At least Alec wasn't. He kept me at arm's length. That was definitely not the behavior of a suitor.

"Now turn over the tiles facing down, but leave them in their positions," Artemis said. "These will reflect possible outcomes."

My hand shook slightly as I flipped over the tiles. I was

more nervous than I realized. "What do they say? Twins and a white picket fence?"

"We already have the white picket fence," Marley pointed out.

Artemis looked thoughtfully at the exposed runes. "Hmm."

"Hmm? That's your interpretation of my romantic future?" I demanded. "Did the genie get a more hopeful outcome?"

"He did not, as it happens," Artemis said. "But that's all I can say about that."

"What do they mean?" Marley asked. "Mom, shouldn't you be able to figure them out?"

Out of the mouths of overachieving babes. "Not yet, sweetheart. Hazel and I are taking it slowly."

"I see conflicting information," Artemis said. "This rune suggests that you will find happiness, but this rune"—She tapped the one to the far left of it—"suggests that someone will constrain you. Test your emotional balance."

"I think everything tests my emotional balance," I said.

"It's true," Marley added solemnly. "What was your exact question, Mom?"

"I'll keep that to myself, thank you very much," I replied. I didn't need Marley getting involved in my love life. It was bad enough she knew as much as she did.

"But this isn't a definite outcome, right?" Marley asked. "Nothing is predetermined?"

"Correct," Artemis said. "Think of the future as a cobweb." She glanced at the chandelier above her head, presumably looking for the giant cobweb that lived there.

"We cleaned, remember?" I said.

Artemis frowned. "In that case, picture a cobweb. The many strands. The interconnectedness of it all."

"Is there a spider?" Marley asked.

"Yes," Artemis said. "The spider is you. Once the spider chooses a thread of the web to climb, she has chosen a path and the resulting vibrations impact all the other parts of the web. She does not choose in isolation."

"And if she doesn't like that path, she can choose another one?" Marley inquired.

"Absolutely," Artemis said. "In which case, the possible outcomes change again."

"I like that version of fate," I said. "That means you're never stuck. There's always a way to improve your situation."

"Yes, it is rather comforting, isn't it?" Artemis agreed.

Beside me, PP3 barked.

"Marley, would you take him outside?" I asked. "His leash is in the carrier."

"Come on, Mr. Peabody," Marley said, scooping the Yorkie into her arms. "Time to check out the possible outcomes of your future pee."

"Jefferson, would you be so kind as to prepare the tea?" Artemis said.

I felt a slight chill as the manservant moved through the parlor room to the kitchen.

"And what was your question?" Artemis asked slyly.

I blinked my eyes innocently. "I can't tell you or it won't come true."

"It's not a wish, dearest. Telling me changes nothing."

"Of course it does," I said. "Telling you impacts the rest of the web somehow. You just explained about interconnectedness and decisions. If I tell you, it could change the outcome."

A slow smile spread across the old witch's face. "And you pretend not to know where Marley gets her sharp mind." She wagged her finger at me. "A werewolf in sheep's clothing, that's what you are."

I gathered the rune tiles and pushed them over the edge of the table, back into the bag. "Like you said, Artemis, it's just one possible outcome and it can change again tomorrow."

And I had no idea what Artemis's information meant. My question was—will I find love again? No surprise that the results were complicated and conflicting. That was basically the story of my life—no casting of runes required.

Artemis patted my hand. "There is no joy without sorrow. No light without darkness."

I snorted. "I thought you were casting runes, not fortune cookies."

Artemis gave me a vague smile. "Just worth remembering. That's all."

CHAPTER 5

I BREEZED into the offices of *Vox Populi* with a death grip on my latte from the Caffeinated Cauldron. I'd had a restless night after a string of dreams about spiderwebs, thanks in no small part to Artemis and her rune-based oracle.

"Rough night?" Bentley asked, vaguely amused.

I tucked a loose strand of hair behind my ear. "Only for the guy I was with." I dropped into the seat at the desk next to his.

Bentley's hands flew to cover his ears. "I don't want to hear the sordid details of your personal life."

"I do," Tanya said eagerly. The office manager fluttered over and perched on the edge of my desk. "Tell me, dear. Was it the sheriff? I bet he's an absolute animal."

I removed my sunglasses. "The only animal in my bed last night was an aging Yorkshire terrier."

"Kinky," Tanya said.

I stared at the older fairy. "I'm talking about PP3, my dog. There was no guy. It was a joke."

Tanya looked crestfallen. "No worries, dear. You're still young. I'm sure things will pick up soon."

"How about that autopsy report on Grover Maitland?" Bentley asked, clearly anxious to change the subject. "Imagine having all that in your system."

I gave him a blank look. "All what?"

"Didn't your boyfriend tell you?" Bentley asked.

I gritted my teeth. "Sheriff Nash is *not* my boyfriend."

"But I heard you were kissing at The Wishing Well," Tanya said.

"Patently false," I said, failing to add that the kissing came afterward. "What was in Grover's system?"

Bentley ticked the items off on his fingers. "Vampire blood, nightshade, and wolfsbane," he said. "You'll need that for the article."

"Gee, thanks," I said. "I wasn't sure whether facts would be important."

Tanya fluttered back to her own desk. "Why do you suppose the sheriff didn't tell you himself? Lovers' quarrel already?"

"We're not…" I heaved a sigh. "He didn't tell me because there was vampire blood." And I knew what that meant. "Anybody know the address for Enders Funeral Home?"

"Is that where the elf's family is having his service?" Tanya asked.

"No," I replied. "That's where the sheriff is probably trying to interview Thomas Enders without my interference."

Tanya called out the address. "It's next to the salon where I get my nails done. I think he uses Ruby, the same nail technician, for the bodies."

I shuddered. "Thanks." I looked around the office. "Where's our fearless leader anyway?" I half expected Alec to appear out of nowhere, as he often did.

"He's at an out-of-town meeting with his agent," Tanya said. "He'll be back tomorrow."

Among his many talents, Alec was also a successful fantasy author. "Oh," I said, a little disappointed that he hadn't mentioned the trip.

"He heard about your night out with the sheriff, you know," Bentley said.

My radar pinged. "Oh? Did he say anything about it?"

"He didn't have to," Tanya chimed in. "I could see the vein in his temple throbbing."

"He has no reason to be upset," I said, especially since he made it clear our relationship was to remain strictly professional.

Tanya pressed her thin lips together. "I know he seems cool and collected, but there is a passionate heart beating in that firm chest of his." She frowned. "Okay, technically there's no heart beating because he's dead, but you understand."

"I understand that Alec Hale is my boss and nothing more," I said. "And the sheriff is..." Truth be told, I didn't know what the sheriff was. We flirted. We kissed, thanks to a mixture of sorrow and alcohol. I had no clue whether it would ever be anything more. I was lucky if I figured out what to make for breakfast without overextending my brain. "The sheriff is in hot water for trying to interview Thomas Enders without me. If you'll excuse me, I'm going to head over there now before he does any permanent damage."

Sure enough, I found Sheriff Nash parked outside Enders Funeral Home. When I tapped on the car window, his head jerked toward me. Nothing like taking the sheriff by surprise. He popped open the door and stepped onto the pavement.

"What are you doing here?" he asked, not entirely pleased to see me.

I crossed my arms. "What do you think?"

"There was vampire blood in his system, Rose," Sheriff Nash said. "Can't ignore the facts."

"There were other substances, too," I argued. "Wolfsbane. Maybe you should interview the entire pack as well."

The sheriff shook his head. "I don't think you understand what wolfsbane is."

"I was just making a point. Besides, you already questioned Thomas."

"Ready for another career change to law, are we?" the sheriff asked. "I barely asked him anything. I was only trying to catch him during an unguarded moment. Thanks to the report, now I have real questions."

"He's innocent," I insisted. "You're wasting your time."

"Great. Then feel free to waste your time out here and I'll waste mine in there. That's probably best anyway. Unless you're in the mood to break another pot, of course."

I scowled. "I'm coming in, if only to make sure you respect his human rights...or his paranormal rights. Whatever they are."

The sheriff held the front door open for me and I shot him a quizzical look.

"I just want to make sure you don't kick me in the rear on the way in," he explained.

Such a gentleman.

Inside, the funeral home was tasteful without being ostentatious. Rich cherry wood furniture and Persian rugs with bold, vibrant colors filled the rooms. The interior looked like the home of someone's well-to-do lawyer friend with a preference for traditional style.

The front door must have triggered a censor or tripped a ward because Thomas immediately emerged from a side room. He smiled when he saw me, but his pleasant expression quickly faded at the sight of the sheriff.

"Good day, Sheriff," Thomas said. "Nice to see you again, Miss Rose. I don't suppose you're here for a tour."

I swallowed hard. A tour of the funeral home? No thanks.

"We'd like to ask you some questions, if you have a few minutes," the sheriff said.

"Of course. I have no appointments until late afternoon," Thomas replied. "Why don't we sit in the lounge where it's more comfortable?"

He returned to the side room and the sheriff and I followed suit. The lounge was every bit as tasteful as the other rooms we'd seen, with mahogany furniture and a large gilded mirror on the wall topped with a carved gryphon.

"The rooms in here are all so beautiful," I said.

"Thank you very much," Thomas said. "I want my clients to feel comfortable saying goodbye to loved ones. The environment is crucial."

"I guess that's why you created a casket for your sand sculpture," I said. "A clever form of advertising."

Thomas shook his head. "Not at all. Like I told you at the beach, I wanted to capture the way I appear when asleep. I'm genuinely interested in that as a form of art. "

At the mention of art, I instinctively glanced at the paintings on the wall. My eyes widened slightly at the image of a fruit basket. "Hang on. Is that one of Trupti's?"

Thomas tapped the pads of his fingers together, pleased that I noticed. "Yes. Do you know her work?"

"More than I'd like," I said. Trupti's fruit paintings came to life recently and I ended up defending myself against an angry banana and his healthy friends. I shuddered at the memory.

The sheriff chuckled. He knew exactly where my mind went. "It's only a painting today, Rose. Nothing to worry about."

I wasn't convinced. I swore the eyes of the fruit followed

me as I crossed the room. Of course, that was impossible because the fruit didn't have any eyes.

That I could see.

"Can I offer you light refreshments?" Thomas asked. "I have a serviceable kitchen here for my guests."

"Nothing for me, thanks," I said. I didn't love the idea of eating or drinking in a funeral home. It made me anxious that I'd end up trapped here forever, like I'd eaten pomegranate seeds in the Underworld.

"I'm good," Sheriff Nash replied. "Can we talk about Grover Maitland now?"

"Of course. Such a shame about the elf," Thomas said, bowing his balding head. Too bad he couldn't have become a vampire when he still had a full head of hair…unless he was a natural born vampire. Either way, it sucked for him.

"Can you tell us where you were on the night in question?" Sheriff Nash asked.

"Still a suspect, eh?" Thomas tapped his chin thoughtfully. "That should be simple enough. I finished my sculpture in the afternoon and then returned here for a funeral. Erasmus Getty."

The sheriff seemed to know the name. "And you were here for the whole event?"

"Absolutely," Thomas said. "That's the job. The family expects me to be at their beck and call, and rightfully so. It's important to feel like you can depend on the someone in times of need."

"What time did the funeral end?" I asked.

"Around ten o'clock," he said. "I remained here until half past eleven. There's always a lot to do afterward."

"Were you alone?" the sheriff queried.

Thomas nodded. "Most of the time. My assistant left around eleven."

"Is that typical?" I asked.

47

"Sometimes the family requests the reception be held here as well. The Getty family chose another venue, so we were finished on the early side."

"And where did you go when you left here?" Sheriff Nash asked.

"Home to bed," Thomas said. "Between sculpting and the funeral, I was exhausted from a long day. I was in my casket until six o'clock the next morning."

"Were you alone at home?" the sheriff asked.

Thomas's expression clouded over. "Yes, I was. And, yes, that *is* typical."

I felt sorry for Thomas. The questions seemed so much more invasive when the paranormal was clearly innocent.

"No alibi," the sheriff mumbled.

"He lives alone," I said. "How's he supposed to have an alibi overnight?" I looked at Thomas. "No talking pets, like maybe a parrot?"

"I'm not Captain Yellowjacket," Thomas said sadly. "Although I do enjoy a good ale at the Whitethorn now and again."

"Too bad you didn't enjoy one there the night of the murder or we wouldn't need to have this conversation," I said.

Sheriff Nash quieted me with a sharp look. "Did you have any interactions with the Maitland boy?"

"I told you at the beach. No, never," Thomas said. "There were plenty of paranormals around when I was sculpting on the beach, but I don't think he was one of them."

"We found vampire blood in his system," Sheriff Nash said. "Can you think of any reason why that would be?"

Thomas's jaw tightened. "You found vampire blood in his system? I suppose that explains why you're here."

"And because you run a funeral home," the sheriff said. "And you're apparently preoccupied with how you look when you're asleep, which is pretty darn creepy, if I'm being honest."

"That's art," I objected.

"Creepy art," Sheriff Nash added. "Maybe you were making creepy art with Grover Maitland and something went wrong…"

"Sheriff," I said hotly.

"I have no interest in boys, Sheriff Nash," Thomas said. "And the suggestion is deeply disturbing."

The sheriff seemed to realize the implication of his remark. "I'm sorry, Enders. I didn't mean it that way."

Thomas waved his hand in the air. "No matter. Water under a troll's bridge. As to your question, vampire blood is used for many purposes, only one of which is turning someone." He peered at the sheriff. "I assume that's what you were wondering—whether I was attempting to turn the boy?"

The sheriff shrugged. "I'm not *wondering* anything. I'm looking for motives. It would be helpful to know all the reasons why vampire blood might be found in a seventeen-year-old elf's system."

"Our blood has healing properties, as I'm sure you know," Thomas said. "The healers use it often in their practice."

"Well, I don't think anyone was healing Grover Maitland," the sheriff said. "Otherwise, he'd still be with us."

Thomas pursed his pale lips. "I'm terribly sorry. I wish I could offer more assistance."

"You've been very helpful, Thomas," I said.

"I still feel terrible that he was discovered in my sculpture," Thomas said. "It gives me a certain sense of responsibility."

"Responsibility?" Sheriff Nash queried.

I jabbed him with my elbow. "It's not an admission of guilt. I think Thomas has answered all of our questions. We should let him get back to work."

"I'm happy to contact you if I think of anything else," Thomas offered.

"Sounds good," I replied, and attempted to steer the sheriff away from the innocent vampire. I knew werewolves and vampires were natural enemies, but the sheriff really needed to check his prejudice at the door if he intended to be impartial.

"I'll return to the beach later if you want to come by," Thomas called. "I do want to make certain my sculpture is holding up now that it's been redone."

I was too busy forcing the biased sheriff out the door to answer.

CHAPTER 6

I STOOD in the woods behind Rose Cottage with Wren, the Master-of-Incantation, working on our weekly lesson. Unfortunately, local chatter about a certain werewolf sheriff and me was interfering with our progress.

"I can't help the gossip mill," Wren said. "Quite frankly, the only way to make it stop is to stop dating him."

"I don't think I *am* dating him," I protested.

Wren cocked his head. "You've been seen out with him on multiple occasions. Under what definition is that not dating?"

"I've been seen out with Bentley and my cousin, Florian. Am I dating them, too?"

"You know it doesn't matter to me one way or another," Wren said. "I know you'll never date a wizard."

I stopped short. "What makes you say that?"

"You're a rebel at heart, Ember," he said. "If Hyacinth insists you date within the coven, I have no doubt you'll be looking to fall in love with a merman or someone equally objectionable."

A merman was objectionable? I filed that factoid away for

future use. "Enough focus on my personal life," I insisted. "Do something useful and teach me a spell I can use on Hazel."

Wren leaned against one of the huge live oak trees and eyed me curiously. "Hazel again? Can't you just humor the poor witch?"

"Come on, Wren," I said. "You know you'd love it if I managed to pull a fast one on that redheaded diva. I can't be the only one she annoys."

Wren suppressed a smile. "Hazel can be...intense about runecraft, I'll say that much. I remember this one meeting where she suggested a runecraft fair as a coven fundraiser." He snorted. "How many attendees would that draw? Five?"

"One simple spell," I begged. "What could go wrong?"

Wren's shoulders slackened, a clear sign he was about to relent. I was giddy with excitement. Hazel would never expect me to retaliate with magic. She thought I was too lazy and incompetent. Ha! I'd show her.

"So you want a spell that mellows her?" he asked, rubbing his square jaw.

"I want her to not tie me to the chair with invisible duct tape," I said.

"Understandable. Maybe something in the vein of an opposite spell would do the trick."

The opposite of Hazel? Now that sounded promising. "I swear I'll do extra credit incantations if you teach me."

Wren extended his wand and pointed it at the live oak tree in front of us. "*Contrarium*."

Before I could blink, the mighty oak tree was reduced to the size of a flower.

That's a mighty fine trick, but it could be dangerous in the wrong hands, a scratchy voice said.

I glanced up sharply to see a raccoon on a tree branch above our heads. "Raoul, what are you doing here?"

Wren's head jerked up. "Who's Raoul?"

The raccoon dangled from the branch by his claws and studied the Master-of-Incantation. *He's good-looking for a wizard. What's wrong with him?*

"Nothing's wrong with him," I snapped. "What makes you think there is?"

You're not flirting or doing that weird thing with your mouth, the raccoon replied.

"I don't do anything weird with my mouth," I insisted.

Wren stared at the two of us, unable to speak.

"Oh, Wren. This is my familiar, Raoul." I snapped my fingers. "Raoul, come down from the tree. It's giving me a muscle cramp to tilt my head at this angle."

You get a muscle cramp when you sneeze, Raoul shot back.

"I get them in my sleep, too," I replied, remembering the night before when I launched myself out of bed with a spasm in my foot. "What else is new?"

Sounds like you need to increase your potassium intake, Raoul said. *More bananas.*

"You're bananas," I said, and turned to smile at Wren. "You've heard me mention Raoul."

Wren's brow lifted. "I remember that you met your familiar. I'd heard he was a trash panda, but I didn't quite believe it."

"He prefers the term rodent bandit," I said.

Raoul swung down from the branch and landed on all fours. *He most certainly does not. He prefers a show of respect.*

"How does your aunt feel about this turn of events?" Wren asked.

It was a fair question. Aunt Hyacinth did not take kindly to anyone disparaging the family name, and a raccoon familiar was definitely fodder for town gossip. I was a Rose, a descendant of the One True Witch. In her mind, my familiar should be as elegant and exquisite as her own, the white furball explosion called Precious.

"She's warming to the idea," I lied.

Wren laughed. "I bet."

"Raoul, you can stay, but you have to be quiet so I can concentrate," I said.

The raccoon pretended to zip his lip.

"You've got him trained to be obedient already?" Wren queried. "Color me impressed."

Raoul unzipped his lip and bared his teeth at the wizard.

"Knock it off, Raoul," I scolded him. I turned my attention to Wren. "If you see foam in his mouth, he's totally faking it. Don't pander to it."

Wren shot the raccoon a cautious look. "Good to know."

Raoul pretended to busy himself with collecting berries from a nearby bush.

"The opposite spell," I prompted Wren.

"Okay, so decide what the object of your spell is, focus your will, and then aim your wand," Wren instructed.

Raoul cleared his throat. *I hope you don't mind me saying so, but he's aiming his wand in your direction right now.*

"He's not holding…" I began.

Not that wand, Raoul said, with a mischievous twinkle in his eye. *His magic wand.*

"Raoul!" I said heatedly.

Made you look, he said, with more glee than any trash panda should be able to muster.

I shook off the interruption and focused on a rock near my feet. I gathered my will, aimed the wand, and said, "*Contrarium.*"

Wren frowned. "What did you do? It's the same size."

"I didn't change the size," I said. I pressed the rock with my toe and was pleased to see its solid nature had softened to a jelly-like substance. "The opposite of hard is soft."

Ha! Raoul said. *Try that spell on his magic wand.*

"Raoul," I said. A warning tone.

What? The raccoon wore an innocent expression. *I meant his real wand this time, pervert.*

Wren touched the rock. "That's really good work, Ember."

Show-off, Raoul said. *I thought you were supposed to be a newb.*

"I am a newb," I said. In all honesty, I was surprised to have gotten it right on the first try.

"We call that beginner's luck, Raoul," Wren said.

"Hey!" I objected.

Raoul chuckled. *Ooh, I'm gonna like this guy. How often do you train with him?*

"Watch your step, Raoul, or I'll be turning you into whatever the opposite of a raccoon is," I warned. What was the opposite of a trash panda? "Hmm. That might work in my favor." I pointed my wand and Wren gently moved the tip downward.

"No taking aim at your familiar," Wren said. "There are rules, you know."

"No, I don't know," I said. "I'm still getting used to the fact that I *have* a familiar."

"I'll bring you a copy of the handbook next time we meet," Wren said. "Ian will be more than happy to discuss it with you." Ian was the Master-in-Familiar Arts.

"Another book?" I lamented. "It's not as ridiculously large as the Big Book of Scribbles, is it?"

Raoul clapped his paws together. *There's a handbook about how you need to be nice to me? It's like Christmas and my birthday at the same time.*

"I bet you don't even know when your birthday is," I said.

Raoul clutched his chest. *Oomph. That was a shot to the heart, Rose. We need that handbook, stat, so I can hit you with it.*

I decided to ignore my distracting familiar. "So I guess

you can't use a spell like this on a dead elf," I said, thinking about Grover.

Wren gave a sad shake of his head. "Afraid not. Necromancy is banned here and the spell isn't remotely powerful enough anyway."

"Necromancy is a real thing?" I asked. I wasn't sure why I was surprised. Nothing should surprise me in Starry Hollow.

"It's a very ancient and dangerous practice," Wren said. "And one to stay far away from. Nothing good ever comes from it."

"So it's like dark magic?"

"I don't believe in categorizing magic in that way, but it's not the type of magic our coven wants to be associated with," Wren replied.

"You don't believe in dark magic?" I queried.

"Magic is only a tool," Wren said. "It's the user that determines whether the magic is light or dark."

"You're not a member of the NRA by any chance, are you?" I asked.

His brow creased. "What's that?"

"Nothing. Forget it."

"How about another try with the opposite spell?" Wren suggested. "Let's make sure you've got it down before using it on Hazel. I wouldn't want it to backfire and get traced back to me." He gave a nervous chuckle.

"Not to worry, Wren," I said, aiming my wand at a toadstool. "As usual, I've got everything under control."

An hour after my lesson, I found myself sitting in a car with Sheriff Nash in the high school parking lot, waiting for the final bell to ring. If anyone saw us lurking here, it would be more fodder for gossip. It didn't matter, though. In my mind, the investigation took priority over idle chatter. Since

Thomas was an undead end, we decided to speak to Grover's best friend and see whether he knew about the unusual substances in the elf's system.

"I've been mulling over the vampire blood," I said. "Even if Thomas didn't try to turn him, do you think there's a chance Grover wanted to be turned?" When I first arrived in Starry Hollow, I'd investigated the death of the coven's Maiden, a young witch called Fleur. She died while trying to transition into a vampire, like her boyfriend. It was a difficult and dangerous process.

The sheriff drummed his fingers on the dashboard. "Hard to say at this point. I would have thought the situation with Fleur would've put anyone off, especially someone like Grover who probably knew Fleur."

"Yeah, that's what I think, too." I paused. "Thanks for inviting me along again." Neither of us mentioned the kiss in front of the cottage.

"Just makes my job easier when I don't have you running around questioning suspects without me."

I couldn't resist a smile. "And you know I will."

His gaze met mine. "That I do, Rose. That I do."

When the final bell rang, we left the car and stood on the sidewalk in front of the school. Marley was staying after school for a piano lesson with the middle school music teacher—a recent development—so I didn't need to worry about collecting her yet. I watched as dozens of students streamed through the open doorways.

"They all look so normal," I mused. Elves, trolls, pixies, fairies, goblins, even a young minotaur. I was already used to the sight of them.

Sheriff Nash cocked an eyebrow. "What do you mean? Of course they all look normal."

I blushed. "I didn't mean it that way. I just can't believe how quickly my brain has accepted all this as reality."

The sheriff's expression softened. "Maybe, deep down, you always knew you belonged in a place like this. You ever consider that?"

"If that's true, I was never aware of it. Normal to me was watching idiot humans weave in and out of traffic on the New Jersey Turnpike. Normal to me was watching kids in hoodies loiter outside of stores because they had nothing better to do."

Sheriff Nash grinned. "We have all that, too. But our idiot drivers have horns and our loitering kids might have wings. We're not so different, Rose."

I shot him an amused glance. "You and me? Is that what you were going to tack on to the end of that statement? You know how Aunt Hyacinth feels about werewolves and witches. They couldn't be more different."

"An abomination, I believe is what she said to my brother when he proposed to Linnea."

I watched a young werewolf lope across the front lawn, oblivious to the dreamy looks of the fairies that congregated by the parking lot. "What were you like as a kid?" I asked. "As cool as that guy?"

Sheriff Nash shook his head. "Much cooler." He glanced at me. "I bet you were sixty kinds of trouble. And loud about it, too."

"Nope, I was as good as gold," I said. "Had my own halo and everything. Used to polish it every Friday night."

"Because you were home alone?" he taunted me.

"I was with Karl, remember?" I said. I'd told the sheriff about Karl, my husband and Marley's father. We'd met in school and married young. Too young. He died four years ago in a trucking accident.

"Ah, yes. Karl, your one and only."

Thanks to some oversharing on my part, the sheriff knew that Karl had been my only sexual experience. I'd opted to remain celibate since his death, focusing instead on making ends meet and raising my daughter. It was only since moving to Starry Hollow and having the pressure taken off me slightly that I'd considered wading into the dating pool, and that was mostly due to Marley's insistence.

"That's the friend we want," Sheriff Nash said, nodding toward a slim teenager with shaggy hair and an oversized backpack.

I squinted. "No pointy ears or wings. What is he?"

"He's a druid," the sheriff said. "He's got healing abilities."

"Is he related to Cephas?" I'd recently met Cephas, the town healer, when there was an outbreak of a disease that brought nightmares—and Trupti's fruit paintings—to life.

"Aldo is his nephew," the sheriff said. "As far as I know, he has a decent reputation. No trouble in school or in the neighborhood. He and Grover were very tight."

"In that case, I'm surprised to see him at school today," I said. "You would think he'd need time to work through his grief."

The sheriff looked at me. "He's a teenaged boy. He's probably trying to prove how tough he is by showing up and acting like it's no big deal."

"Because that's what you would've done?" I queried.

"I probably would've shown up drunk, but I'd show."

"Yoo-hoo," I called, waving him over. "Aldo. Can we talk to you for a quick second?"

The sheriff glanced at me. "Yoo-hoo?"

I shrugged. "It's an expression."

"If you're an owl."

"No, that would be who-who," I said.

Aldo approached us, his hands jammed into his pockets. He looked like a typical teenager, complete with a hoodie and flashy green sneakers.

"I guess you want to ask me about Grover," Aldo mumbled.

The sheriff squinted at me. "Did you catch any of that, Rose? I don't understand Mumblese."

"Well, you speak it perfectly fine," I countered. "Yes, Aldo. We'd like to talk to you about Grover. How are you holding up?"

Aldo blinked in surprise. "I figured you'd want to interrogate me or something."

"We'd like to ask you a few questions," the sheriff said, more gently than his usual gruff tone. "But, like Miss Rose, I'd like to know you're doing okay first. This has got to be a tough time for you, losing a close friend."

Aldo struggled to contain his emotions. "It hasn't been awesome, that's true."

"Have you been able to talk to anyone about it?" I asked. "A counselor or maybe a family member?"

Aldo wiped his nose on his sleeve. "My Uncle Cephas. He's good with stuff like this."

"Yes, he's a good choice," I said. "He seems very compassionate."

"Druids tend to be compassionate," Aldo said. "We carry a lot of responsibility in the healing community."

"Are you planning to train as a healer when you graduate?" the sheriff asked.

"Yep," Aldo said. "It's the only thing I've ever wanted to do. That's why Uncle Cephas and I are so close."

We beckoned Aldo away from the group of teenagers that had assembled nearby. We didn't want the conversation overheard by any gossiping students.

"Do you know any reason why Grover would've had vampire blood in his system?" the sheriff asked.

Aldo's head snapped to attention. "Vamp blood? Are you for real?"

"We're for real," the sheriff replied.

Aldo frowned. "If he had vamp blood in his system when he died, shouldn't he have become a vampire?"

"It's not that simple, Aldo," the sheriff said. "You'll learn more about that when you study as a healer. We also found nightshade and wolfsbane in his system."

Aldo coughed a response.

"I didn't catch that," the sheriff said.

Aldo's expression grew pinched. "Those are poisons, right?"

"Yes, Aldo. They are deadly," I said. "Grover must have suffered. If you know anything at all, now's the time to spit it out."

"He had an argument with one of our teachers recently," Aldo said. "I saw the whole thing. She was pissed at him."

"I thought Grover was a good student," I said.

"It was something about a paper he turned in," Aldo said. "I've never heard her talk like that to anyone before. She's usually super nice."

"What's the teacher's name?" the sheriff asked.

"Miss Cranshaw," Aldo replied, and my heart skipped a beat.

"Maisie Cranshaw? The history teacher?" I asked.

"That's right," Aldo said. "She's a pixie."

I looked at the sheriff. "She has a sand sculpture in the competition. The castle."

Sheriff Nash nodded. "Thanks for your input, Aldo." He clapped the young druid on the back. "You keep talking to your uncle whenever you feel the need, you got it?"

"I will," Aldo said. "Will you tell me when you know more about Grover?"

"Promise," I said.

CHAPTER 7

Hyacinth Rose-Muldoon swept into the office in one of her usual kaftans. The bright yellow number she sported today was adorned with images of white, fluffy cat heads.

"They look like daffodils," I said, inclining my head toward her kaftan.

"They most certainly do not," my aunt objected. She tapped one of the cat faces on her chest. "They are quite clearly designed to look like Precious."

"If you say so," I mumbled.

My aunt stared down her nose at the broken pieces of Jimmy, the garden gnome that I'd placed on the desk in her office. "And what is this you've brought to me?"

"A favor," I said. It occurred to me that I probably shouldn't have insulted her kaftan first. "May I present Jimmy?" I gestured to the pieces like they were game show prizes to be won. "Can you do a spell that puts this garden gnome back together exactly as it was?"

Aunt Hyacinth peered at me. "It's called glue, my dear. No magic required."

"No, you don't understand," I said. "This is a very special gnome and I need it to be the same as it was. If I glue it, they'll see the cracks and it will be awful."

"Who are *they?*"

"The Maitlands," I replied.

Recognition flickered in her eyes. "The family of the dead elf."

"Yes. I broke the gnome and it turns out that Grover gave it to his mom for Mother's Day." I knew that would be a persuasive piece of information.

Sure enough, my aunt fixated on the gnome. "The boy's last gift to his mother?"

"It was. She was devastated when I showed her what I'd done. I need to give it back in one real piece or I'll have ruined this woman's life. There has to be a spell, right?"

My aunt touched the pottery fragments. "Of course there is, darling. I'm a Rose, aren't I?"

"Well, technically I'm a Rose, but I don't know any spells for this."

"In time, my dearest Ember," my aunt said, and patted my cheek. "Why do you think I'm so intent on supplying you with the best teachers?" She paused. "Speaking of which, how are you progressing with your studies? Hazel says you have a strong resistance to runecraft. Why is that?"

Because Hazel is a crazed clown hell-bent on destroying me with the Big Book of Scribbles? "It's not so much resistance as distracted by other things."

Aunt Hyacinth regarded me carefully. "Distractions like Granger Nash?"

Here we go. "Distractions like covering Grover Maitland's murder for *Vox Populi*, your newspaper."

"I understand you've been spotted out with the sheriff several times now." She plucked a fragment of Jimmy from the desk and pretended to study it in the sunlight. "I expected an update from you long before now."

I swallowed hard. "An update? Why would you expect that? I'm not a spy." On myself, no less.

She set the piece back in the pile and met my incredulous gaze. "I made it very clear to you how I feel about your romantic prospects. They should be limited to the Silver Moon coven. A wizard worthy of a descendant of the One True Witch. Wren would be an excellent match for you."

I groaned inwardly. "And I made it clear to you that I'm a grown woman and I will date whomever I choose and I don't need your permission to do it."

Aunt Hyacinth tapped her coral-colored fingernails on the desk. "How badly do you want this gnome restored to his former glory?"

I sucked in a shocked breath. "You wouldn't."

"I'll do whatever is necessary to protect the family name," she replied. "I thought you understood that."

"Think of Dottie Maitland," I begged. "This is the last remaining link to her son. What if this was from Florian?"

She cast a withering glance at the gnome. "If this monstrosity were from Florian, I would question his love for me."

"Kinda missing the point," I said.

Her shoulders relaxed. "Fine. I'll restore this without any strings attached out of the kindness of my maternal heart."

"Thank you."

My aunt closed her eyes and focused her will.

"No wand?" I queried.

She opened one steely eye and focused it on me. "Not for a witch of my ability. Now hush, my dear." The eye shut and she held her hands over the broken gnome. She uttered a few Latin phrases I couldn't quite make out. Sparks shot from her fingertips and I took a self-preserving step backward.

The pieces began to whirl in the air like they were caught in the vortex of a tornado. They moved toward each other and fused together. Finally, Jimmy the garden gnome appeared on the desk as though he'd never been kicked across the concrete.

"Thank you so much," I said, and reached for the gnome. My hand knocked against his hat and tipped it over, spilling the contents. Wait, what contents? I lifted the clear bags from where they'd fallen on the desk. "What are these?"

My aunt's eyes widened. "Put it down. Now."

I dropped the bags onto the desk. "What's wrong? Did the spell go sideways?"

She blew air from her nostrils. "No, my spell did not go sideways. I am not an amateur. Those bags contain deadly substances."

I blinked at the bags on the desk. "Like drugs?"

"Deadly as in poisonous." She pointed to the first bag. "That's nightshade."

My breathing hitched. "And let me guess. The other one is wolfsbane."

She gave me an admiring glance. "Well done, Ember. Someone is teaching you, it seems."

"The autopsy report found nightshade and wolfsbane in Grover's system. I don't understand where these bags came from. They weren't in there before."

My aunt clasped her hands together. "They were at some point. My magic was not a simple repair spell. I used a combination of spells, one which involved an element of time travel."

"Time travel," I repeated.

"We can't use it on living creatures," she explained. "Only objects. I restored the gnome to his former glory by plucking it out of another moment in time."

"And that moment in time happened to involve deadly plants," I said.

"Apparently so."

I set the hat back on Jimmy and scooped him off the desk. "I'll take him to the Maitlands, and then I'll bring these bags to the sheriff."

"Just take care with the bags," my aunt advised. "I wouldn't want you to accidentally expose yourself to these substances. Even skin contact can be problematic."

"So sweet that you care," I said.

"Of course I care," she snapped.

Her motivation was plain. "Because I'm a Rose?"

She appraised me coolly. "Can you think of a better reason?"

I entered the library and waved to Delphine Winter behind the desk. The librarian also happened to be a member of the coven and one of Marley's favorite paranormals. No surprise that my daughter gravitated to the woman with superior book knowledge.

"Nice to see you, Ember," the librarian said. "Where's my favorite customer?"

"She's having dinner with her cousins tonight," I replied. Bryn and Marley were thick as thieves and Linnea enjoyed having Marley over to act as a buffer between Bryn and Hudson.

"Are you picking up books for her?" Delphine asked. "I don't remember seeing any on reserve."

"No, I'm not here for Marley," I said. "I've got another project in mind."

"Will I see you at the coven meeting this month?" Delphine asked.

"You're going?" I inquired. Delphine wasn't the most involved Silver Moon witch. She tended to keep to herself, preferring books to paranormal interaction.

"I decided to make more of an effort," she said, twisting a strand of hair around her finger. "Do you think Florian will be there?"

Ah. Now it made sense. "Of course. His mother would hex his butt if he skipped a meeting. She takes coven business very seriously."

Delphine nodded solemnly. "As she should."

"If you do decide to show up," I said, lowering my voice, "maybe dab on a little gloss. Florian has a thing for shiny lips." I wasn't sure if that would be enough to grab my cousin's ever-shifting attention, but it was a start.

Delphine lit up like a Christmas tree. "Thanks for the tip."

I continued through the library lobby and headed upstairs. I didn't bother to look for Maisie in the fiction section. Based on our conversation at the beach, I knew where to find her. Sure enough, I recognized her iridescent wings as she browsed titles on the top shelf of the history section.

"Maisie?" I called.

From the next row over, a voice shushed me. "Too loud," someone said in a stage whisper.

Modulating the volume of my voice was *not* my specialty.

"Hello there," Maisie said, appearing to recognize me. "You're the reporter, right?"

I felt a surge of pride at the mention of my job title. Most days I still expected to be cursed at, spit on, or chased, such was my previous life as a repo agent.

"Yes," I replied. "Ember Rose."

Maisie drifted to the floor, a thick book in her hand. "Doing a little research?"

"Yes, but not the same kind you're doing. I'm here to talk to you about Grover."

Her expression clouded over. "Poor Grover. Such a tragedy. He was a nice young elf. He was a student in my American history class, you know."

"That's actually why I'm here," I said. "I understand you argued with Grover recently. Can you tell me what that was about?"

Maisie stared at me. "Who told you that? I don't want that printed in the paper. The whole incident is particularly awful now that he's dead."

"I'm not looking to report on it," I said. "I only want to piece together Grover's last few days. It's my understanding that he was a good, quiet kid, so I was surprised to hear he'd argued with one of his teachers, especially when I heard it was you. It seems out of character."

Maisie's guard dropped. "You're absolutely right. It *was* out of character. In fact, the whole incident wasn't like Grover at all. I think that's why I reacted so strongly."

"What happened?" I asked. From another row, a voice shushed me again. "Okay, okay," I called over the top of the shelf. "Don't get your cloak in a twist."

"I asked to speak with him after class to discuss his paper on Lord Pumpernickel."

"Lord Pumpernickel?" I echoed. I couldn't claim to be an expert on American history, but I had no recollection of a Lord Pumpernickel.

Maisie gave me a patient smile. "He was a vampire in the South during the Revolutionary War. He was the reason Lord Cornwallis surrendered."

"Ah. The paranormal history version."

"That's right. You should think about taking a class or two at the local community college," Maisie suggested. "It would be nice for you to learn more about your heritage."

"I'm sure Marley will tell me all about it," I said with a laugh. "That's my daughter. She has an insatiable thirst for knowledge and is always happy to share." Whether I wanted to sleep or not.

"A budding scholar in the family," Maisie said. "How marvelous." Her brow creased. "I wish I could say the same about Grover. I was so disappointed when I realized he'd plagiarized another paper. He was never an outstanding student, mind you, but he always did the work. Lately, I'd noticed that he'd slacked off. It started with missed homework assignments and then the plagiarized paper. I decided to talk to him about it after class."

"And how did he react?"

"Not well, as you can imagine," Maisie said. "He was surprisingly defensive. Not his usual calm self. I wasn't sure whether it was because he was afraid I would tell his parents or something else. He just seemed more belligerent than I was expecting."

"And did you speak with his parents?" The Maitlands didn't mention any problems at school when the sheriff and I visited.

"I didn't have the chance," she replied. "I had planned to, but I took time off for the sandcastle and had intended to speak with them when I came back to work."

"So when someone claims you had an argument with him, he was the one actually arguing with you?" I queried.

Maisie nodded. "He denied plagiarizing it. I could tell he was sleep deprived. He had dark circles under his eyes, which wasn't typical for him. With his recent missed homework assignments on top of that, I assumed there might be family drama. That's often the case. Maybe a divorce in the works?"

"That certainly wasn't my impression of the Maitlands," I said. But something to consider. "So how did you leave things with Grover?"

"I gave him the opportunity redo the paper on his own," Maisie said. "I knew Grover wasn't a bad kid. I wanted to give him another chance." Her gaze lowered to the floor. "Obviously, that won't happen now."

No, it wouldn't. Sadly, Grover Maitland was all out of chances.

CHAPTER 8

BEFORE RETURNING Jimmy to Mrs. Maitland, I decided to research where Grover may have purchased the ceramic gnome. I had no way of knowing what timeframe my aunt used when she restored it with the spell. What if the deadly plants had been in the pot when Grover bought it? Maybe he'd hidden the bags, thinking they were recreational drugs and discovered the hard way they weren't. Or maybe the bags had ended up there when the teens pranked each other.

I started with Paradise Found. It was the largest garden center in Starry Hollow and I figured it would be simple enough to throw the Rose name around if necessary and get answers. I felt mildly ridiculous, preparing to whip out my identity like I was Superman disguised as Clark Kent. Then again, the Rose name had clout in Starry Hollow and, if it helped me find the killer of a young elf, then so be it.

Most of the garden center was outdoors and I quickly realized it was arranged like a maze. Each section of the maze contained a different variety of plants, trees, shrubs, and flowers. There was a delightful madness to the arrangement.

"Can I help you find something?"

I whirled around. "Oh, it's you. I should have known." It was the middle-aged man with receding brown hair who'd designed the maze sand sculpture.

He smiled when he recognized me. "You're the witch from the newspaper. I'm Adam Forrest." He offered his hand and I shook it.

"This is your garden center?" I asked.

"It is. My pride and joy." The way he beamed at the mention of it, I didn't doubt it for a second.

"Is that why you chose a maze for your sculpture?" I asked.

Adam nodded. "I loved the idea of sculpting a smaller version of this maze out of sand. A wonderful challenge."

"Do you have a minotaur here, too?" I joked, thinking of the buff sculpture in the middle of the sand maze.

"Only a real one," Adam said. "My business partner, Frederick."

I attempted to disguise my shock. "So the sculpture was modeled after Frederick?" And, if so, where was this amazing creature with the buns of steel now?

"It was," Adam said. "He's the perfect specimen in my eyes. Too bad for me he's partial to women." He chuckled to himself. "Luckily, we've managed to maintain a wonderful friendship, as well as a productive professional relationship."

As hard as I tried, I couldn't figure out which type of paranormal Adam was. "Are you a wizard? I haven't seen you at any coven meetings."

"That's because I'm a sorcerer," he replied. "Different magic."

"Ooh," I said. "I think you're the first sorcerer I've met."

"We don't run about in large numbers like witches and wizards, that's for certain," he said. "And we don't have covens, so we tend to live a more solitary lifestyle."

"There are times I can see the appeal of that," I replied, thinking of my aunt.

He laughed. "So what brought you here today, if not my sand sculpture?"

I removed Jimmy the garden gnome from my tote bag. "Any chance this little guy was purchased here?"

Adam didn't hesitate. "There's every chance. I sell many gnomes like that. They're locally made and I try to support local businesses whenever possible."

"Is there any way to verify it?" I asked. "A serial number or something?"

He rubbed his chin. "I'm afraid not. Why the interest in this gnome?"

"At one point, this little guy housed nightshade and wolfsbane," I said. "I'm trying to determine whether he left the garden center with those items in his hat or whether they were stored there later."

Adam recoiled. "I keep a wide variety of plants here, but I can assure you that deadly ones are not part of the mix. As a sorcerer, I am acutely aware of the dangers."

"So these gnomes aren't being used to distribute illegal substances?" I asked. "Maybe they're brought in from outside Starry Hollow and transported to customers this way?"

Adam grimaced at the suggestion. "Absolutely not. The gnomes are locally made, as I said. I think I'd know by now if I was supplying half the town with deadly poisons." He paused. "And I think the sheriff would know by now as well."

"Which local company supplies the gnomes?" I asked.

"Sierra," he replied. "She owns Sierra's Ceramics. Not the friendliest woman in the world, but she runs a good business."

"Does she supply garden gnomes to the whole town?"

"Her gnomes travel much farther than Starry Hollow," he said. "She's very successful."

I glanced at the gnome in my hand. He didn't look particularly special, but, then again, I wasn't into ceramic figures of any kind.

"Will you be attending the sand sculpture ceremony next week?" Adam asked.

"Definitely," I said. "I'm covering it for the paper, remember? I've got to be there for the announcement of the winners. I honestly don't know how they'll choose. There are so many good ones."

"I can't imagine what it'll be like next year," Adam said. "I suspect the competition will be more intense now that we know what to expect."

"I don't how you'll top the maze," I said. "The minotaur alone is worth a prize."

"I'm inclined to agree with that statement," a deep, rumbling voice said.

"Frederick, so glad you're here," Adam said. "This young lady is a reporter for *Vox Populi*."

I turned around and craned my neck for a decent view of the incredibly tall and muscular man in front of me. Adam wasn't kidding about that sculpture.

Naturally, the first thought that came to mind shot from my lips before I could stop myself. "Where are your horns?"

He smiled down at me, seemingly unoffended. "This is my human form. When you're as large as I am, it makes it easier to get around town."

At the mention of his size, my gaze drifted to inappropriate places and I immediately snapped my head up. "I guess the horns are tough in a car."

"I do have a convertible, but I don't always like to drive with the top down," he admitted.

I stuck out my hand, completely enthralled by this giant. "I'm Ember Rose, by the way."

He wrapped his hand around mine and it felt like my

entire body was being covered in a warm blanket. "Frederick Simms. My friends call me Rick, except Adam. He prefers Frederick."

"He really does," Adam said.

"Where are you from, Ember?" Rick asked. "You don't look familiar."

"New Jersey," I said. My neck began to ache from gazing up at him. "You've probably never heard of it."

"Are you kidding?" His expression brightened. "Bon Jovi, Bruce Springsteen, Bruce Willis, Tom Cruise. New Jersey is a hotbed of talent."

"I'll forgive you for Tom Cruise because you're so incredibly…tall," I said.

His laughter was like a roll of thunder. "I've been to the Jersey shore. Do you know Point Pleasant?"

"You haven't been there looking like this," I said. "You'd be on the news." Or his own reality show.

"I shrink down a little for the human world," he said. "Not my muscles, though. I like to keep those."

"I can see why." It was hard not to ogle him. Whereas Sheriff Nash had a scruffy, masculine charm and Alec had a dapper beauty, Rick was raw animal magnetism. I could understand Adam's disappointment in having zero chance with him.

"Miss Rose was asking about Sierra," Adam said.

Rick winced. "Oh no. You haven't had a run-in with her, have you? She's a bit rough around the edges, that one. Likes to get her drink on at the Whitethorn on Thursday nights. It's not a pretty picture." He shuddered.

"I haven't met her," I said. "I was asking about her garden gnomes."

Rick seemed to notice the one in my hand for the first time. "Yes, that's definitely one of hers. I recognize her work."

"Thanks," I said. *Popcorn balls.* His eyelashes were thick enough to braid.

"Is there anything else we can help you with, Ember?" Rick asked. "Maybe we could talk about it over coffee over at the Caffeinated Cauldron?"

My mouth opened but no sound came out. I couldn't possibly go out with this guy. I'd committed to a lifetime of no dating since my husband died, yet here I was in Starry Hollow, already entangled with a werewolf and a vampire. Could I possibly add a minotaur to the mix? That was pure lunacy. My aunt would ring for her smelling salts.

A slow smile curved my lips at the thought of my aunt's apoplectic reaction.

"As a matter of fact, I would love a coffee," I said, smiling brightly.

"So why on earth were you in New Jersey?" I asked.

Rick and I sat in a booth in front of the double-fronted window for all passersby to see. I fervently hoped this sighting didn't kick the rumor mill into overdrive. My 'special relationship' with the sheriff was bad enough.

"I traveled up to New York City to see a friend," he said. "Made a few stops along the way."

Inwardly, I giggled at the thought of Rick riding the subway in his minotaur form. New Yorkers would probably be too busy staring at their phones to notice him.

"Is there a paranormal section of the city?" I asked. It never occurred to me there might be pockets of paranormal life within larger human cities.

"There are several, as it happens," Rick said. "I was in the Starlight district, near Soho. Best Italian food on the eastern seaboard."

"That's high praise," I said, although I knew some South Philly Italians that would take issue with his statement.

"Ember, what a delightful surprise."

I turned around to see a familiar face behind me. "Montague! How great to see you." In the middle of the day and sober, no less. The elderly wizard moved aside to reveal the woman standing behind him.

"Hello, Ember," she said.

"Daffodil?" I glanced from the witch back to Montague. "You're here together?"

Montague took Daffodil's weathered hand in his. "We are," he said. "We come this time every week. It's part of our new routine."

It seemed that showering was part of his new routine as well. He looked and smelled like a respectable wizard should.

"How's Libby?" I asked. Libby was his late wife's familiar. He'd been neglecting the cat as well as himself, and I was optimistic for a good report.

The couple exchanged happy glances.

"Libby lives with me now," Daffodil said. "She's a wonderful cat. I couldn't have asked for a better companion."

"I take exception to that," Montague said with mock outrage.

She leaned over and kissed his wrinkled cheek. "I stand corrected."

Behind me, Rick rose to his full height and I watched Montague's eyes grow round at the sight of the minotaur.

"Rick, I'd like you to meet my friends, Montague and Daffodil," I said.

Rick offered a huge hand to the kindly wizard. "Ember and I are just getting acquainted."

Daffodil gave him an appraising look. "Is that so?" She inched closer to me and whispered, "Good for you, dear."

I opened my mouth to object but didn't want to insult Rick.

"I'm confused," Montague said, scratching his head. "I heard you were dating the sheriff."

Rick placed that huge hand on my shoulder. "Really? Granger's got himself a girlfriend?"

I closed my eyes and wished myself far away, but no dice. I desperately needed to learn a teleportation spell like the one my cousins used to bring me to Starry Hollow. If they could do it, then so could I.

"I'm not his girlfriend," I said, clenching my fists. "I'm not anyone's girlfriend." If this kept up, I was going to start wearing a T-shirt with that same declaration.

"Well, I'm Montague's girlfriend and I don't care if the whole town knows about it," Daffodil said. She radiated joy and I felt a surge of warmth. *Good for them*, I thought.

"You should stop in for lunch one of these days," Montague said. "You won't recognize my place since the last time you were there."

No doubt. Montague had left his deceased wife's belongings intact as though she'd still been living there. It had been painfully sad.

"I would love to," I said.

"She should come to my house," Daffodil said. "More room and she can see Libby. Bring that sweet daughter of yours."

"Even better," I said. "Marley adores cats."

Daffodil winked. "That's to be expected with a young witch."

I wasn't so sure about that. There was no guarantee Marley would inherit anything more than my dark hair and blue eyes. She had her father's stubborn chin, so there was every chance she'd inherited the human genes.

Montague and Daffodil continued to the counter to place their orders.

"They seem nice," Rick said.

"I know, right? They've infected me. I'm definitely nicer here than I was in New Jersey. I haven't called anyone a jackass since I've been here." *To their face.*

"I bet you were much kinder than you think," Rick said.

We'd only settled back into our chairs when Thaddeus came thumping through the coffeehouse. The centaur worked for the Starry Hollow Tourism Board and had been crucial to Florian's success with the sand sculpture competition.

"Ember, I thought I spotted you in the window," Thaddeus said.

Not to self: no more window seats. "Hi, Thaddeus. How's it going?"

He pushed his glasses to the bridge of his nose. "Time for my late morning burstberry tea. Everyone needs that one thing to get through the day."

"Mine is thistle and fennel tea," Rick said. "Very calming."

"Yes, yes," Thaddeus said. "An excellent suggestion." He peered at me over the rim of his glasses. "How's the investigation? Florian says you're working alongside the sheriff again. Getting to be a habit, eh?"

Rick draped his impressive arm along the back of his chair. "I thought you were a reporter."

"I am," I said. "I was covering the sand sculpture competition, but once I discovered Grover Maitland's body, the story took a turn."

"*You* discovered the body?" Rick seemed aghast.

"My daughter and I," I said.

"Yes, I heard someone mention a daughter," Rick said. "How old is she?"

"Ten," I replied. "Her father died a few years ago." I wasn't sure why I felt compelled to add that sad nugget.

"I feel terrible for the Maitlands, obviously," Thaddeus said, "but I can't help but feel sorry for Florian. He worked so hard on this event and now all the attention has turned negative."

"I know," I said. "I had the same thought."

"Some of the local attractions are rejoicing. They were unhappy with the competition's popularity," Thaddeus said. "I overheard Lotus complaining in the Wish Market."

Lotus was a witch in charge of the popular broomstick tour in Starry Hollow. "Why would Lotus be unhappy?" I asked. "I would think the competition's popularity is good for the whole town."

"In a sense, but nobody likes to lose revenue," Thaddeus said. "Apparently, her numbers were way down from last year and she blamed the competition."

"But the broomstick tour is amazing," I said. "I can't imagine a short-term competition could do much damage to an evergreen attraction like that."

Thaddeus wiped his glasses with a plaid handkerchief. "You'd be surprised."

"You're a witch," Rick said. "What's so amazing about the broomstick tour?"

"I don't have my broomstick license," I said. "I didn't know I was a witch until recently. When I said I was from New Jersey, I should have specified the human world."

The realization hit the minotaur. "Oh, I remember now. You're the missing Rose girl." He wagged a finger at me. "You're kind of a big deal."

My back straightened just a smidge. "I don't know about that."

"Don't be modest," Rick said. "A descendant of the One True Witch is nothing to sneeze at." He scrutinized me. "You don't have that telltale white-blond hair, though."

Instinctively, my hand flew to touch my hair. "I don't have a lot of their attributes."

"You have more than you think," Rick said. "Besides, the darker hair suits you."

He was certainly generous with the compliments, much more forthcoming than the sheriff or the closed-off vampire. It was a nice change of pace.

"Thanks," I said. "And those muscles suit you." The words tumbled out before I could stop them.

Thaddeus snorted at the look of horror on my face. "No worries, Ember. Nobody would argue with that."

"So do you really think the owner of the broomstick tour would be upset enough about the sand sculptures to murder someone?" Rick asked. "Because that's mafia-level business."

At the mention of the mafia, I flinched. The whole reason I lived in Starry Hollow stemmed from an incident with a known mobster. James Litano's effort to kill me triggered my magic, which then allowed my trio of Rose-Muldoon cousins to locate me.

"You okay, Ember?" Rick asked. "Did I say something wrong?"

I forced a smile. "No, you make a good point." I sipped my drink. "Still, I think it's worth having a little chat with Lotus." At least it would be an excuse to do the tour again. Until I got my broomstick license, the tour was my only option for taking flight.

"This has been fun," Rick said. "How about we do it again sometime?"

My cheeks grew flushed. Before I could respond, Thaddeus reached across me with a slip of paper.

"Here's her number," he said. "She has a fairly packed schedule, so weekend nights are best."

I gaped at the centaur. "When did you become my personal assistant?"

"Between you, Florian and Aster, I know the schedule for the entire Rose-Muldoon clan for the rest of the year." He leaned toward me. "Don't forget Sunday dinner at Thornhold. Bring a small hostess gift this time. It's considered polite."

"Um, thanks for the tip."

Rick grinned as he tucked the paper into his pocket. "I'll be in touch."

"No touching," I said, too quickly. "Just a phone call. Or a text."

The minotaur chuckled. "I'm so glad I walked into that maze today. Totally worth it."

CHAPTER 9

THE SHERIFF WAS NOT AS KEEN as I was to follow up on my lead from Thaddeus. His boots were propped up on the desk in his office and he gazed at me over the top of them, trying to decide if I was serious or not.

"You're suggesting that Lotus, a respected witch in *your* coven and the owner of the broomstick tour, killed a teenaged elf and buried him in a sand sculpture because she didn't like competing for attention?"

I cringed. "Well, when you put it like that, it does sound silly, but you said yourself that we can't always understand why paranormals choose to commit the crimes they do. It's our duty to explore every avenue."

"Technically, it's *my* duty, but I take your point." The sheriff shifted his boots to the floor, seeming to acquiesce. "You know what, Rose? You're right. Maybe the broomstick tour is the only thing Lotus has ever done that she's proud of. And now its position as a top destination in town is under threat. It's at least worth a conversation."

I didn't expect him to cave so easily. "Really?"

He cocked an eyebrow. "You want me to change my mind?"

I tossed him the car keys from the corner of his desk. "Nope. Let's go."

Deputy Bolan stuck his head in the doorway. "Do you need me, Sheriff?"

"Not for this one, Bolan," he replied. "Rose and I have it covered."

Deputy Bolan scowled at me, at least I thought it was a scowl. His leprechaun face was so tiny, sometimes it was hard to tell.

"Maybe we should get a badge made for her," the deputy suggested. Although I heard the sarcasm, the sheriff apparently didn't.

"That's not a bad idea, Bolan," he replied. "But her reporter credentials are probably good enough. We don't want to encourage her now, do we?" Sheriff Nash winked at me, completely missing the look of disgust on his deputy's face.

"No, we certainly don't," Deputy Bolan replied. "Let me know what you find out."

The sheriff grinned. "Will do."

We arrived at the tour around lunchtime, and my first thought was that the tour was closed. There seemed to be no one around, a sharp contrast to the assembled crowd the last time I was here. I leaned over to the sheriff. "Are we here officially or are we undercover?"

The sheriff grinned. "You'd like that, wouldn't you? A little roleplay?"

I nudged him with my arm. "I'm not talking about that. I mean…"

He chuckled. "I always know what you mean, Rose. It's one of your charms."

I glared at him. "Oh, now I have charms? When did that miracle occur?"

He eyed me appreciatively. "Come now, Rose. You know better than that."

We approached the ticket window and I gave the paranormal a big smile. "Two tickets, please."

The sheriff balked. "Why are we getting tickets?"

I flashed him an innocent look. "Why do you think? We're going to take the tour. I did it once with Marley and it was awesome."

The sheriff shook his head. "I'm too busy for this. Let's just talk to Lotus and be done."

"It's important research," I insisted.

"No, talking to Lotus is important research," he countered.

Understanding dawned on me. "You're afraid of heights."

"No, I'm not," he said, a tad too defensively.

I jumped up and down in an extremely mature fashion. "You are!"

"Fine," the sheriff said, jamming his hands into his pockets. "So I don't want to fly around on a broomstick. Big deal. I'm a werewolf, not a witch. My feet belong firmly on the ground."

"Sheriff, you don't know what you're missing," I said. "The broomstick tour is incredible. You see the whole town from a new vantage point."

"I can see the town perfectly fine from the top of the Lighthouse," he replied. "Remember? We ate there together once. I shared my soup."

"It's not the same," I said. "Flying over the town is a completely different experience. You have to do it to understand it. I'll be practicing for my broomstick license soon. This is a good opportunity to get started."

The paranormal handed me two tickets and I gave one to the sheriff. "We're going. No arguments."

The sheriff snatched the ticket from my fingertips. "Has anyone ever told you you're bossy?"

I smiled. "All the time. If you're a good wolf, maybe I'll let you share my broomstick."

The sheriff seemed to like this idea. "Front or behind?"

I fluttered my eyelashes. "Whichever way you like it."

His throat tensed at the suggestion.

Unlike my visit with Marley, there was no wait this time, so the sheriff and I went straight over to select our broomstick. Fortunately, Lotus was there. She seemed pleased to see the sheriff ready to partake in the tour.

"The sheriff on the broomstick tour. This has to be a first," she said. "Miss Rose, I hope you're covering this for the paper. Such great publicity."

I shot the sheriff a knowing look. If Lotus was this excited about favorable publicity for the tour, maybe she was capable of more extreme measures.

"I wouldn't think you're in need of any publicity, Lotus," I said. "You do a great business here. I see your broomsticks flying overhead every day." That much was true. I was accustomed to them now, but initially I found myself holding a handbag over my head in case someone thought it would be funny to spit.

Lotus frowned. "I know, but sales have been dramatically down because of that blasted sand sculpture competition. It seems like no one is interested in broomstick tours. It's hurting my bottom line. Not to mention my reputation as the number one destination in Starry Hollow."

"Well, there's nothing like a dead body to put off paranormals," the sheriff said. "I have no doubt the number of visitors to Balefire Beach has dropped since the discovery of Grover Maitland."

Lotus heaved a sigh. "That was very sad news. Grover was a wonderful young elf. He worked here over the summer and I got to know him a bit. I have nothing but good things to say about him."

The sheriff regarded her with renewed interest. "The victim worked here over the summer?"

She nodded. "That's right. Once school started, he got a job elsewhere. I don't need the extra hands during the low season, so I always expect to lose a few part-timers."

"And when was the last time you saw Grover?" the sheriff asked.

Lotus looked thoughtful. "Last week. He was hanging around the pier with that group of friends he's always with. There's something odd about that group. I didn't love when they came to see him in the summer."

"Really? Why not?" From what I knew, they were all good kids. Not a troublemaker in the bunch.

Lotus chewed her lip. "It's nothing I could put my finger on. We all get vibes now and then, don't we? I know you must, Miss Rose." She glanced apologetically at the sheriff. "Maybe it's a witch thing."

The sheriff shrugged. "I've been known to get vibes on occasion," he said. "I happen to prefer facts, but when my gut speaks, I listen."

That made two of us.

"Did you ever notice them doing anything suspicious?" the sheriff asked.

"No, nothing out of the ordinary," Lotus replied. "Like I said, it was just a feeling that something wasn't right with them. There was a strange intensity if that makes sense."

I wondered whether she was being genuine or whether she was simply trying to throw us off her trail.

"Well, the good news is that the time for the sand sculpture competition is limited," I said. "That must make you happy. Business will be back to normal before you know it."

"That's my thinking as well," she said. "My only concern is that it's so successful, they might decide to do it multiple times a year. There are all sorts of ways they could expand on the idea. And no offense to your family, Miss Rose, but I'm sure they've been ecstatic to finally give Florian something useful to do."

She wasn't wrong. In fact, I was beginning to think that she was more astute than deadly. The sheriff must have had the same thought because he held up the broomstick.

"Where should we return this?" he asked.

I blinked. "Return it? We haven't used it yet."

He gave me a hard look. "I think we're probably done here, Rose. Wouldn't you agree?"

I thrust the broomstick against his chest. "Not on your life, Sheriff. Buckle up, cowboy. It's going to be a bumpy ride."

"You're going to pay for this, Rose," he growled, as we walked to the edge of the dock where the tour began.

"And I'll enjoy every moment of it," I said.

We listened to the instructions and the sheriff took his place behind me on the broom.

"Nice view," he said.

I craned my neck to look back at him. "We're not in the air yet."

He gave me one of his lopsided grins. "That's not the view I'm talking about."

My body warmed at the compliment. I handed him the leather strap attached to the broomstick.

"I didn't peg you for a leather girl," he said.

"You steer," I said.

"And here I thought you were the alpha."

"My broomstick is bright red with the Silver Moon flag

flying at the back," Lotus said. "Not that it matters. I'll be the only one flying with you today."

"That's what I call service," the sheriff said. "It's the VIP treatment."

"Indeed," Lotus said, sounding disappointed. She clearly missed her large tour groups.

As we followed Lotus into the air, I heard a sharp intake of breath behind me.

"You okay, Sheriff?" I yelled.

"Yep. Peachy."

"Are your eyes open?" I asked.

"Don't insult me, Rose."

"They're closed, aren't they?"

"Maybe."

I laughed. He was as bad as Marley.

I marveled at the view of the ocean below as a pod of dolphins surged through the waves. "Look!" I yelled.

"In a minute," Sheriff Nash said.

"You'll miss it if you wait." I couldn't turn around to see whether he'd opened his eyes.

"Nice fish," he said.

"They're mammals," I said. "Marley would have a conniption if she heard you say that."

"Your hair is tickling my nose," the sheriff said. "Can't you do a spell to keep it in place?"

"You overestimate my abilities," I called over my shoulder. "Over there! The statues in the fountain are moving." I felt giddy with excitement as the seven statues changed positions.

"They do that every day," the sheriff replied.

"But you don't get to see it happen from up here," I argued. We swooped over the Silver Moon headquarters with its statue of a witch holding a moon above her head as though it were a beacon.

"Hey, your witch is barefoot," the sheriff said. "Did you know that?"

"I noticed that last time," I replied.

"Why don't you wear one of those head things," he said.

"A circlet?"

"Yeah, that. It'd look pretty with your dark hair."

"Sheriff Nash, I think that's one of the nicest things you've ever said to me."

"You're a natural on a broom. How about that? Is that even better?"

"You're scoring a lot of points right now," I said. "That's for sure. There's Fairy Cove!" I pointed to the curve of the shoreline.

"And the Lighthouse," the sheriff said. "Where we had our first date."

"That was not a date," I objected.

"We ate together. Alone."

"We'd just interviewed the chef of the restaurant and you were hungry," I said. "That doesn't qualify as a date."

The broomstick ahead of us turned, so we turned, too.

"Please tell me we're heading back to the dock now," the sheriff said.

"We are," I said. "You can unclench now."

We glided onto the dock without a single bump. The sheriff staggered off the broom and dropped to his knees.

"Thank Mother Nature," he breathed.

"You were fine up there," I said.

He glanced up at me. "I'm much better now." He patted the dock with both hands. "This is where a werewolf belongs, Rose."

"A dock next to the ocean?"

He growled. "On land."

Lotus came to stand beside us. "Anyone need a nausea potion?"

The sheriff waved her off. "I'm good." He dragged himself to his feet. "Thanks for the tour, Lotus. That was a once-in-a-lifetime opportunity."

She laughed. "Hardly. We're open every day of the year, including holidays."

"Not for me." The sheriff swaggered off the dock and I hurried after him.

"I didn't realize how much you'd hate it," I said. "You didn't have to prove you weren't afraid, you know."

He stopped and looked at me. "I didn't do it to prove I wasn't afraid."

"Then why did you do it?"

"Isn't it obvious? To prove how much I like you, Rose." With those words, he continued to the car. I stared after him, uncertain how to respond.

"Thank you," I said quietly.

CHAPTER 10

I'D JUST FINISHED a spell on my crockpot when I heard scratching at the kitchen window.

"What are you doing, Raoul?" I asked, crossing the room to open the window. "Can't you come to the front door like a normal...raccoon?" A statement I never imagined myself making back in my New Jersey apartment.

I don't do doors, he replied. *I'm strictly a window animal.*

"There's no such thing as a window animal. Dressing, yes. Animal? No."

He climbed onto the counter and looked at me. *Do you want to hear what I have to say or not?*

"That depends. Does it involve stolen goods? Because I don't want to be identified as an accessory."

That's insulting! I'm not a thief. He paused. *Anymore.*

"Fine," I said. "Out with it."

I know you're asking around about the elf, he said. *I was... foraging and overheard two pixies expressing severe displeasure over the sand sculpture competition. Like it was ruining their lives.*

I leaned my back against the counter and studied him. "When you say 'foraging,' do you mean trash picking?"

Raoul narrowed his dark eyes. *Such judgment in your voice. Okay, so maybe I was hitching a ride to the dump.*

"You're kidding, right?" I looked askance at my raccoon familiar.

Raoul shrugged his furry shoulders. *What can I say? At least I'm consistent.*

"And you heard these pixies complaining about the sculpture competition?"

Were they ever! It was like listening to a time loop. The same complaints over and over, Raoul replied. *I got so bored, I climbed off the back of the truck and went to the park instead. I love a good ride to the dump. That shows you how annoying it was.*

"Well, let's go find these trash pixies," I said.

Raoul shook his head in disgust. *I'm sure they prefer sanitation pixies. Where are your manners?*

I got into the car and was surprised when Raoul climbed into the passenger seat.

"What do you think you're doing?" I asked. I watched with interest as he settled in beside me.

What? I'm coming with you. We're a team.

"We are not a team," I insisted. "Sometimes I work with the sheriff, but that's the only furball I'm willing to work with."

Why? Because you're hungry for the wolf? Lame." He made the L sign with his claws.

"First of all, the song is Hungry *Like* the Wolf," I corrected him. "If you're going to reference Eighties music, get it right. Second of all, I do not need a raccoon trailing me all over town. It looks strange."

If it weren't for this raccoon, you wouldn't have this lead.

I sank against my seat. "Fine, but you have to wear your seatbelt. I'm not getting a ticket because of you. Deputy Bolan would be thrilled to cite me."

I waited to start the car until he snapped himself in. As his claw reached for the radio, I smacked it away.

"I control the music," I said. "Radio, play…"

Welcome to the Jungle, Raoul interjected.

"Hey! This radio won't respond to you because…" I didn't get to finish my sentence as the beginning strands of *Welcome to the Jungle* began to play. "How did you do that? I thought I was the only one who could hear you."

It's your magical radio system, Raoul said. *You and I have that psychic connection, so the radio can hear me, too.*

I started the car and inched down the driveway. "Great," I grumbled. It was bad enough sharing the radio with Marley, who objected to my love of Eighties and Nineties music. Now I had to compete with Raoul, too. At least he'd chosen an Eighties song, even though the band wasn't one of my favorites.

We drove all around Starry Hollow, scouring the streets for the pixies in question. We caught up with them as they began their daily cleanup of Balefire Beach, appropriately enough.

I parked the car and observed the pixies zipping around the beach, collecting debris. They were incredibly fast. The perfect paranormals for a job like this. I cast a sidelong glance at Raoul.

"Are pixies faster than fairies?" I asked.

No question, Raoul replied. *Pixie wings are designed for speed. Fairy wings are more decorative, although they can fly with them.*

I observed the pixies for another minute before venturing over to the beach. I slipped off my shoes and carried them in my hand. It was such a pain to get remnants of the beach out of my car. There had to be a spell for that.

I waved to the pixies. "Hey, guys," I called. "Got a minute?"

They halted in midair and looked at me suspiciously for a brief moment. Then they sped over to me with such force that I worried the breeze would knock me over. Luckily, I managed to stay upright.

"Hi," I said. "I'm Ember Rose and I'm covering the sand sculpture competition for the weekly paper."

The blond pixie rolled his eyes. "This stupid competition is the bane of my existence right now."

"Mine too," the other pixie said. "It's the pits."

"Is that so?" I asked. "What's the problem?"

"The cleanup is taking twice as long every day," the pixie explained. "We're falling behind on our daily schedule. The boss doesn't like that and we keep getting in trouble. Joel here had his pay docked because he was caught taking lunch when he should have been working."

"And Billy here has had to work overtime every day since the competition started," Joel added.

I looked from one pixie to the other. "Wait. Your names are Billy and Joel?"

"That's right," Billy said. "We've been on the same sanitation team for five years now."

I broke into a broad smile. "You have no idea how happy that makes me."

"I already thought you were weird for walking around with a raccoon," Billy said. "Now I'm convinced."

I squinted at them. "You guys have never heard of Billy Joel?"

The pixies exchanged confused glances.

"Nope," Joel said. "What team does he play for?"

I clutched my heart. "He's not an athlete. He's a musician. *Piano Man? We Didn't Start the Fire? Uptown Girl?*" They gave me blank looks. "Oh, this is a genuine tragedy." Never mind the murder I was investigating. "I'll fix this in a few minutes. First, I need to ask you a few questions."

"We heard about the elf," Joel said, "if that's what you want to ask about. We weren't here when the body was discovered, though."

"No," Billy said, "I heard it was some nutjob with the hots for the sheriff."

I balled my fist. "I think your informant is inaccurate. I heard it was a beautiful young woman with the voice of an angel."

Raoul choked back laughter.

"Is something wrong with your raccoon?" Billy asked. "Maybe he's got a hairball."

I am not a cat, Raoul objected vehemently.

It's no use, I said to Raoul telepathically. *They can't hear you*. To the pixies, I said, "He's fine. He just needs more fruit and vegetables in his diet."

"Have you complained to your boss about the volume of work that's been created by the competition?" I asked.

"Can't," Joel said. "He'll just replace us with another team. Balefire Beach is the best gig. We don't want to give it up."

Billy nodded. "We had to wait a couple years until the last team got fired so we could get this section of town. We don't want to give it up, but the sand sculptures have been a real headache."

I studied him. "How much of a headache?"

"Me and Joel have both said we hope it flops, so that they don't do it again," Billy said. "We want to discourage it however we can."

"Is that so?" I asked. "And how would you make sure that it flopped? I guess a dead body in one of the sand sculptures would take care of that."

The pixie cocked his head at me. "Man, that's a dark statement, lady. I guess you see a lot of bad stuff as a reporter." He looked at his friend. "Maybe she's got the PTSD."

I stiffened. "I do not have *the* PTSD. That's not even how you say it."

Joel gave Billy a knowing look. "I think you might be right. We're talking about docked pay and overtime and she's talking about murder. Cray cray."

"There are all kinds of motives for murder," I said hotly. "Maybe you didn't even murder the elf. Maybe you found the body in a dumpster somewhere and decided to move it to the sand sculpture in order to solve your own problem instead of notifying the authorities."

Raoul elbowed me. *That's a really good theory. They could totally have found a body in a dumpster.*

I ignored him. "You never know what someone is capable of. Everyone's limits are different."

Billy and Joel inched away from me.

"The worst thing I ever found in a dumpster was…Well, you don't want to know," Billy said. "It was disgusting."

"The worst thing I ever found in a dumpster was a body, but he was alive," Joel said. "He was beat to a bloody pulp, though. I took him to the healer's office in my truck."

A good sanitation Samaritan. It figured. I got the distinct impression these pixies were not willing to go to deadly lengths to stop the competition. "Do me a favor, will you? Keep an ear out when you're cleaning up. If you hear anything suspicious about the elf's death, let me know, okay?"

"Sure thing," Billy said. "And I'd like to have a listen to that guy's music that you mentioned. What was his name again?"

I stared at him. "Billy. Joel."

Joel burst into laughter. "That's us."

I sighed inwardly. "Come over to my car for a minute, so I can enlighten you."

The pixies fluttered beside me as Raoul and I returned to the car. I slipped inside the driver seat and turned on the engine. "Radio, play *Scenes from an Italian Restaurant.*"

The upbeat song began to play and the pixies listened

eagerly. Their expressions brightened as the song continued.

"I like it," Billy said, once the song finished. "It's real peppy and it has a story. I like stories in my music."

Joel nodded. "Puts an extra flutter in your wing."

"You should listen to more of his music when you get a chance," I said. "He would be great for singing along to while you're working." I remembered how often I sang along to Billy Joel when I was working as a repo agent, waiting for my moment to strike. Billy Joel got me through a lot of menial tasks in life.

"Thanks for the introduction," Billy said. "I'll definitely let you know if we hear something."

"As much fun as this has been, we've got to head out," Joel said. "We've been in enough trouble this week and we need to head back to the dump now."

I saw Raoul's face light up at the mention of the dump. "Hey guys," I said. "Would you do me a huge favor and let my friend ride with you? He's a huge fan."

Billy chuckled. "Trash heaven for the trash panda, am I right?"

Raoul danced a little jig. He was so excited, he didn't even object to being called a trash panda.

"Look, it's like he knows," Joel said.

"You're welcome," I whispered to Raoul. I pulled out of the parking lot and headed home, singing along to Billy Joel the whole way.

I sat alone in the offices of *Vox Populi,* typing up everything I'd learned so far about Grover and the suspects we'd ruled out. I was so immersed in my work, the sound of the front door startled me. A familiar little elf entered the office. She glanced around the empty room warily before her gaze settled on me.

"Cindy?" I queried. "It's Cindy, right?"

Grover's little sister broke into a smile, seemingly pleased that I remembered her. "I was hoping you'd be here," she said.

"What can I do for you?" I expected her to mention something about a class project involving journalism, in which case I would promptly direct her to Bentley's desk to leave a note.

Instead, she said, "I want to talk to you about my brother."

My eyebrows shot up. "Oh. I'm sorry, but I don't have any new information for you yet."

Cindy glanced around furtively. "No, but I have information for *you*."

I wasn't expecting that. I hunched over to listen. "Fire away, kid."

"This is off the record," she said somberly.

"Of course," I replied. "But if it might help catch your brother's killer, then why not tell the sheriff?"

She chewed her pink lip. "Because I don't want to get Grover's friends in trouble. They're already upset about him. The last thing they need is the sheriff getting involved."

Uh oh. I tried to maintain a casual air. "So what kind of bad stuff are his friends involved in?"

Cindy fidgeted with the bobblehead troll on my desk, a gag gift from Bentley. "I don't know exactly, but Grover had been coming home late the past few months. I mean really late."

"And that was unusual?" I asked. For a teenaged boy, it didn't sound unusual. I knew they were wired differently. Hell, I'd been married to one. Karl used to wake up at two o'clock in the morning, play a quick round of a video game, and then come back to bed. I laughed at the memory. We'd been so stupidly young to be married and have a child.

Cindy dropped the troll on the floor and bent down to pick it up. "Whoops. Sorry. Yes, he never used to do that.

Mom and Dad didn't notice, though. Mostly, he'd sneak out after they went to bed."

"But you were awake?" I queried.

"I have sleep issues," Cindy said. "Always have. I take magical melts to get to sleep, but there's nothing to keep me asleep. I usually wake up four times a night, if I'm lucky."

"What are magical melts?"

"Little pills that melt in your mouth. They have a potion inside that tells my body it's time for sleep, but I still wake up a lot."

Ugh. That sounded like torture to me. "There's nothing anyone can do for you?"

She shrugged. "My parents took me to various specialists over the years. We've traveled to see sleep healers. It seems to be one of those things. The healers say, as long as I'm healthy and functional, that it's not a problem. I just don't need as much sleep as a normal elf."

"So you'd been hearing your brother come and go in the night," I repeated. "Do you know where he was going?"

"Somewhere with Jordy, Aldo, and Spencer," Cindy said.

I cocked my head. "How do you know which friends he went out with if he came home alone?"

"I checked his phone one night after he was asleep." She gave me an innocent look. "What? I had nothing else to do and I wanted to know what he was up to. I'm the little sister. I needed bribery material."

I folded my arms. "And?"

"They talked about some kind of out-of-body experience," Cindy said. "I think they were experimenting with drugs."

That made sense. "Do you know where his phone is now?"

"Mom gave it to Sheriff Nash," Cindy said. "But you won't find any of the messages. They were all deleted."

"Again, how do you know?" I asked.

"Because I'm the one who got it off the front step. I checked the messages before I handed it over to my mom. They were wiped clean."

"The front step?" I echoed. "What was it doing there?"

Cindy splayed her hands. "Beats me. It turned up there after he died."

Someone was with him when he died and kept his phone. Why risk leaving the phone on the front step when they could've been seen? Why not toss it somewhere it would never be found, like Billy and Joel's dump?

"There aren't any surveillance cameras around your house, are there?" I asked.

"No way," Cindy replied. "Grover never would've snuck out all the time if there had been." She held up a finger. "And don't mention it to my parents. I don't want them installing one before I'm old enough to sneak out."

I placed my hand over my heart. "I promise I won't. Any chance you're interested in a career as a journalist when you're older?"

Cindy's face glowed like a new moon. "I would love that. It's my dream."

"Keep up the nosiness then, Nancy Drew," I said. "It's working for you."

She scrunched her cute little elf nose. "Who's Nancy Drew?"

"You're not familiar with the mystery stylings of Nancy Drew?" I was aghast. "Your next port of call is the library, Cindy Maitland. Look up Carolyn Keene as the author, even though she wasn't a real person."

"She wasn't?" Cindy asked. "Was she a paranormal?"

"No, but I think Bella Forrest might be," I replied. If Cindy didn't know Nancy Drew, she probably wouldn't recognize Bella Forrest either.

"Ooh, *A Shade of Vampire*," Cindy said. "I love that series."

"Cindy, you're too young to be reading those books," I said. "Do yourself a favor and check out Nancy Drew. There are loads of books. They'll keep you busy when you can't sleep."

Cindy beamed. "Thanks, sounds great."

"Now tell me about Grover's friends. I've met Aldo. Who are Jordy and Spencer?"

"Jordy is a nymph. She's super pretty, but doesn't care about that, which is cool. Spencer is a satyr." She wrinkled her nose like a bunny. "He's annoying, but Grover liked him. He was always wearing these dumb crystal necklaces and talking about chakras."

"They certainly sound like an interesting circle of friends," I said. "What do you think they had in common?"

"Acne and homework," Cindy shot back, and I nearly choked on my saliva. "That's about it."

"Jordy doesn't sound like she suffers from acne," I said. Not if Cindy viewed her as 'super pretty.'

"I guess not," Cindy relented.

"Where can I find this odd bunch?"

"Jordy plays matchball most days after school," Cindy said. "She's a superstar. Spencer lurks everywhere. I swear that guy has no purpose."

"He's a sheep?" I queried.

"No, I told you," she said. "He's a satyr." She shook her head in amusement. "There's no such thing as a weresheep."

"Why not?" I asked. "There seem to be shifters for everything else."

"No," Cindy said. "There are no werejellyfish."

"Thank goodness for that." I tried to imagine those wobbly bodies roaming around Starry Hollow and shuddered.

"Why don't you know this stuff?" Cindy asked. "I thought journalists were supposed to be smart."

"I'm smart in my own special way," I replied smoothly. Brutal honesty from children was okay in my book.

She studied me intently. "Did you grow up here?"

"No, as a matter of fact, I grew up in the human world," I said. "A place called New Jersey."

She recoiled. "The armpit of America?"

"Hey!" I objected. Okay, this form of brutal honesty was unacceptable. "It's a lovely place." If you liked traffic congestion, crime, and high property taxes.

Cindy leaned her elbows on the desk. "What's it like?"

"Have you ever been to the human world?"

"Nope. We talked about going to see sleep doctors in Raleigh or somewhere in Virginia, but Mom and Dad said my being an elf would raise a red flag."

"You can say that again," I said. "Sticking to paranormal towns is a better plan." An idea occurred to me. "You know what, Cindy? My daughter goes to the middle school and she's nosy *and* a big reader. I bet the two of you would hit it off. Would you be interested in coming over after school one day, if it's okay with your parents?"

Cindy vibrated with excitement. "I'll ask them, but I bet they'd say yes. They're always too busy with work to pay attention to what we're doing anyway."

I winced. Cindy didn't even sound disappointed when she said that. Apparently, the same problems plagued paranormal *and* human families.

"You can always have your mom call and leave a message for me here," I said. "Tanya is an excellent office manager." When she was actually in the office.

"Great," Cindy said. "I can't wait."

A lead on Grover's murder and a potential playdate for Marley. No one could say I wasn't a multi-tasker.

CHAPTER 11

"Right this way, Miss Ember. Everyone is waiting," Simon said. It was time for our weekly Sunday dinner at Thornhold, the Rose family's grand estate. My aunt's butler gave Marley a friendly bow. "Miss Marley."

"Here." I thrust a small box into Simon's hands.

Simon appeared perplexed. "You brought a hostess gift this time?"

"It's considered polite," I said, echoing Thaddeus's statement from the coffee shop.

Simon smiled. "Certainly. I'll deliver this to my lady."

"I love your glasses, Simon," Marley said. "Are they new?"

Simon's smile widened. "As a matter of fact, they are." He tapped the arm. "A friend suggested that perhaps the old pair didn't suit me."

I gulped. Simon couldn't read minds like vampires could he? Because I was certain my initial thought upon meeting him was that his glasses only served to make his bald head appear rounder. I was inclined to agree with his friend— these black rectangular frames were a huge improvement.

"They're very nice," Marley said.

"Ditto," I added, to assuage my guilt over my unkind thought.

"You'd think there'd be a spell to cure bad eyesight so you didn't need glasses at all," Marley mused on our way into the dining room.

"Maybe that's an area you can focus on when you're older, Miss Marley," Simon said. "New spells are always in the works, not all successful, of course."

I ruffled her hair. "Cool. You'll be a magical scientist." Assuming she came into her witch powers. Ugh. I dreaded her next birthday.

"Finally," my aunt said. "I was beginning to think we'd need to release the hounds."

"Ha. Funny," I said faintly, because I wasn't entirely sure she was joking. Knowing my aunt, she had a pack of hellhounds at her disposal for just such occasions as a tardy niece.

I was surprised to see two additional guests at my aunt's table for our regular gathering. Sunday dinners were usually restricted to family.

"Alec's here," Marley said happily. My daughter was a big fan of Alec's, both the author and the vampire.

Alec pushed back his chair and stood when we entered the impressive dining room. Every time I came for dinner, I was reminded that my entire apartment in New Jersey could fit inside this one room. It never ceased to take my breath away. Between the huge oval table, the magical chandelier, and the family crest over the fireplace, I felt like I was dining with academics from Hogwarts—that, at any moment, a giant hat might appear and sort me into a different family. Not Marley, of course. In my eyes, she was as perfect as any Rose. Instinctively, I glanced at the dark blue banner that hung above the mantel. The Rose family crest featured a full moon and stars with a red rose in front of the moon. It was undeniably beautiful.

"Good evening, Miss Rose," he said politely. "Miss Marley."

Marley beamed like she'd been granted her witch powers a year early. "Can I sit in the empty seat next to Alec?" she asked my aunt.

"Of course, darling," Aunt Hyacinth replied. "You'll make an excellent dinner companion for him."

No doubt. The only remaining seat was across from Alec and next to…"Wyatt?"

The werewolf grinned. "I know, right? I have to admit, I was kinda shocked myself to get the invite."

"Mother and I agreed that it would be nice to include you again once in a while," Linnea said from further down the table. "The children specifically requested it."

"I did," Hudson said. "Bryn said she didn't care either way."

Bryn elbowed her younger brother in the ribs. "I said I didn't *mind* either way. There's a difference between not minding and not caring, knuckle-dragger."

"I'm not a knuckle-dragger," Hudson shot back. "You must be confusing me with your boyfriend."

"First of all, gross," Bryn said, wrinkling her nose at the notion. "Second of all…"

"You have a boyfriend?" Linnea and Wyatt asked simultaneously.

"No," Bryn said in a huff. "Hudson's being a goober."

Wyatt pulled a bowl of mashed potatoes toward his plate. "Time to dig in yet? I'm starving."

"One moment, please." Aunt Hyacinth rang her little silver bell and the rest of the platters floated into the room and set themselves on the table.

Wyatt rubbed his hands together. "Everything looks delicious."

"His approach to food is basically his approach to women," Aster said, and Linnea glared at her from across the table.

"Now, Aster," Aunt Hyacinth said. "We don't need to raise unpleasant topics at the dinner table. You know better than that."

"And in front of our children," Linnea added.

"And in front of me," Wyatt interjected, although he didn't seem particularly upset by the remark. Probably because he knew it was true.

My aunt lifted her flute. Time for the family toast.

"*Carpe noctem*," we said in unison.

Alec's lips stretched into a smile. "Ah, yes. Seize the night. I'd forgotten that was your family motto. An excellent choice."

"You would think so, wouldn't you?" Wyatt said.

"I would think werewolves favored eventide as well," Alec said.

Wyatt scrunched his nose. "Don't go getting fancy on me, vamp. I'm not in the mood to Google 'eventide.'"

"Use your context clues," Marley said, completely in earnest.

Wyatt turned his scrunched nose in Marley's direction. "What kind of clues?"

Aster heaved a sigh. "Just drink from your flute, Wyatt. And do try not to dribble."

Wyatt made a show of pouring the bucksberry fizz down his throat in one go.

"Any updates on the investigation, Ember?" Florian asked, in an effort to take control of the conversation. "The competition ends soon, but no one's talking about it anymore. They're too concerned about the murder."

"That's understandable," Linnea said. "If there's a killer running around targeting teenaged boys, we *should* be concerned."

"I don't know that one death means there's a killer targeting teenaged boys," Aunt Hyacinth said.

Bryn grabbed her brother by the shoulder. "Take Hudson next, whoever you are."

Aster cleared her throat. "Maybe we shouldn't talk about murder at the dinner table." She jerked her head toward her two sons, Aspen and Ackley.

"The sand maze is so cool," Aspen said. "I'm glad nobody died in there."

Wyatt shrugged. "We don't know for sure that he didn't die in there. He could've been killed in the maze and then the body was moved to the casket afterward."

"Wyatt!" Aster hissed.

Aspen's eyes rounded at the thought. He looked at his mother. "Can we go back to the maze? I want to look for blood."

"That's enough, Aspen," Sterling said firmly. Aster's husband gave Wyatt a sharp look. "Let's put a lid on the cauldron, shall we?"

"I'd like everyone here to go to the beach for the winner's ceremony," Florian said. "We need to keep the focus on the competition."

"I agree," Aster said. "It's important to the tourism board that this competition is a success."

"And it's important to me," Florian said. "I finally managed to do something productive. I don't want it overshadowed by…an unfortunate incident."

"Well, if we don't want to discuss updates on the murder investigation, how about an update on you and my brother, Ember?" Wyatt asked. "Can't say I was shocked when I saw you two canoodling at the Wishing Well."

My back straightened. "We were not *canoodling*," I said hotly. "We were commiserating. And who says canoodling anyway? You're not a Hollywood tabloid."

Wyatt shrugged. "You say commiserate. I say lick each other's faces off." He heaped another spoonful of mashed potato onto his plate.

Alec cleared his throat. "That sounds like quite an interesting evening."

My cheeks burned. "There was no licking of any kind."

Aster rolled her eyes. "Mother, was including Wyatt in our dinner plans really such a good idea?"

Wyatt held up his hands. "Hey, I wasn't responsible for licking anyone that night. My tongue was firmly in cheek."

Hudson snorted with laughter as his mother groaned.

"I don't think you understand that phrase," Marley said.

"The sheriff and I are friends," I interjected. "He was bothered by the…unfortunate incident. So I joined him for a drink to talk about it."

"*A* drink?" Wyatt asked. "Or a few drinks?"

"What's the difference?" I asked. "It was perfectly innocent either way."

"After a few drinks, you might misremember how innocent it was," Wyatt replied.

"Yes, Wyatt's the expert on that," Aster said.

Linnea pointed a finger at her younger sister, ready to strike back with magic.

"Don't you dare," Aster said, eyeing the trigger finger.

I tossed back the rest of my drink and tried to keep the steam from pouring out of my ears, cartoon-style. I really needed a spell to keep Wyatt in line. I was so mortified, I avoided eye contact with Alec all together. It wasn't like I was dating either one of them, but I still felt self-conscious about the implication.

"Girls, no magic at the table," Aunt Hyacinth warned.

"Wyatt, I think it's high time we left Ember well enough alone, don't you?"

Finally. What took her so long to step in? Usually she was in there with a backhanded compliment or a Southern-style putdown before anyone could draw breath.

"Jonnie Rastelli got expelled from school today for dropping glitter bombs from the second floor," Hudson said. "One landed on Mr. Peters."

Linnea laughed. "The gym teacher? Isn't he a satyr?"

Hudson nodded gleefully. "You should've seen him. He was so red, you could see it straight through all the glitter. And then there was a trail of glitter all the way to the teachers' lounge."

There was an audible sigh of relief as the topic shifted. While the chatter turned to school hijinks, my mind was still focused on Wyatt. He was such a perpetual thorn in my side. I thought of the spell Wren had taught me and wondered whether it would be worth trying it out on Wyatt before I took aim at Hazel. Nature knew the whole family would thank me for getting us through dinner without further trouble from Wyatt. And his kids would be happy because he wouldn't be tossed out on his backside, which still felt like a real possibility to me.

He sat right beside me. I could do the deed without anyone noticing. As discreetly as I could, I slipped my wand from my waistband. I focused my will, pointed my wand at the offending werewolf under the table, and opened my mouth to murmur the magic word. At the last second, Precious leaped onto my lap and knocked the tip of the wand a good ninety degrees. For a brief moment, I thought she'd ruined the spell, until Wyatt spoke.

"Linnea, your hair has never looked better," he said. "It's the color of the full moon. How I miss stroking it in the evenings."

Linnea's features softened. "Thank you, Wyatt. That's very sweet."

"It's a Rose trait," my aunt said, patting her own white-blond chignon. "It isn't exclusive to Linnea."

"Not all Roses," I reminded her.

"No, indeed," my aunt replied, her disappointment evident. "Have you considered coloring it?"

My hand flew to my dark hair. "Absolutely not. I'd look ridiculous with light hair."

Aunt Hyacinth scrutinized me. "True. Your complexion would be completely washed out."

"I think you could get away with any color, Miss Rose," Alec said.

Gallant vampire to the rescue. "Thank you, Alec, but I'm sure my aunt is right. I've got freckles, too, which doesn't help." Whereas my Rose cousins all enjoyed flawless skin. They were like walking, talking pieces of art and I was the toddler's fingerpaint equivalent.

Thanks to my secret spell, the rest of the meal went off without a hitch. Wyatt was on his best behavior and no one seemed suspicious. They probably assumed it was down to Hyacinth's reprimand.

"I'd like to say goodbye to my ex-wife before I go," Wyatt said, once everyone had gathered in the foyer after dessert. "Tell her how beautiful she looked tonight and how much I miss her honey and lemon scent."

Next to me, Alec said, "That's kind of you, Wyatt. I'm sure she'll appreciate the sentiment."

When Linnea emerged from the downstairs bathroom, Wyatt blocked her path. "Would you mind if I came by and helped make dinner one night this week? I'd like to spend more quality time with you and the kids. I miss you all so much."

"Yes," Hudson said, and fist pumped.

"You actually want to help make dinner?" Linnea queried. "Not just eat it?"

"I also want to fix that railing you told me about," Wyatt said. "Although I'll never understand why you don't use more magic."

"Because too much magic is exhausting," Linnea said. "I've always told you that."

"It's time I start listening, right?" Wyatt said. "I've never been a good listener. It's one of my worst flaws. I spend too much time thinking about my own needs and disregarding everyone else's."

Linnea stared at him, stupefied. "Better late than never, I suppose."

"How about I escort my family home to Palmetto House?" Wyatt asked. "It's already dark." He tossed a smile over his shoulder at Alec. "Or eventide, as some might say so elegantly."

"That's very considerate of you, Wyatt," Linnea said, unable to hide her surprise.

"Thanks, Dad," Bryn said.

"Where's the lady of the house?" Wyatt asked. "I need to thank her for such a nice meal."

Although everyone stared at the werewolf, no one dared say a word and risk ruining the moment.

As if on cue, my aunt appeared in the doorway. "You're quite welcome, Wyatt. If you keep up these manners, we just might have you back."

"Yes, ma'am," he said, and offered his arm to Linnea. "My beautiful former bride."

Once the four were out of the house, Aunt Hyacinth smiled. "See what a little hospitality can do? That's a good lesson for us all right there."

A little hospitality and a little magic, I wanted to add, but I kept quiet about my spell. I didn't want anyone to know what

I'd done. For one thing, I didn't want to cause trouble for Wren. The whole point of learning that spell was to use it as a practical joke on Hazel, not revenge on Wyatt for being a wereass. Plus, I had no idea whether the spell lasted until I reversed it. I needed to ask Wren.

"What a pleasure to see Wyatt in such generous spirits," Alec said. "He's rather charming when he sets his mind to it."

"I agree," I said. "I wonder what got into him." I tucked my wand further into my cloak pocket.

"Who cares, as long as it continues?" Aunt Hyacinth said. "Goodnight, everyone. Lovely to have you, Alec. You know you're welcome here anytime. Impeccable manners, as always."

I knew from experience that wasn't strictly true. Telling Alec he was 'welcome anytime' was in the same vein as 'let's do lunch' or 'how are you?'

"It's always an enjoyable evening at Thornhold," Alec said, with a little more enthusiasm than he typically demonstrated. Technically, my aunt was his boss, so a little ass kissing was to be expected.

"Have a good night, Alec," I said.

He stood and extended his hand. "Why don't you walk me out? It's such a clear night. Perhaps we'll see a few constellations."

"Um, sure. Why not?" I walked with him as far as the driveway.

"I'll see you at the office bright and early tomorrow, yes?" Alec asked.

"I won't have time tomorrow," I said. "I've got a packed schedule." Runecraft homework, a vet appointment for PP3, Cindy's lead to follow up on, a psychic skills class, and a stop at the Wish Market because I promised Raoul I'd pick him up a slug parfait, which was apparently a delicacy in certain circles.

Alec flashed a proud smile. "You're very impressive, Ember. You've stepped into these new roles with the greatest of ease. Your family must be very pleased."

"I guess so."

Alec gazed at me with a look I'd never seen him wear before. If I wasn't mistaken, it looked like...adoration.

"I'd very much like to kiss you goodnight," Alec said.

"I know, but you won't," I said.

His fangs dropped down. "Won't I?" He reached around my waist and pulled me closer. His lips were warm and inviting against mine. I didn't even mind the gentle scraping of his fangs. I was so wrapped up in the kiss, even if he drew blood, it was doubtful I would've noticed.

When he finally released me, I stared at him, dumbfounded. "Is this because of what Wyatt said about his brother? Because we were *not* canoodling in the bar." And no one knew about our kiss outside the cottage.

"My behavior is not dictated by Granger Nash," Alec said.

Maybe not, but I was sure it gave the vampire a little motivation. I didn't wait for him to dismiss me with his usual 'goodnight, Miss Rose.' Instead, I beat him to the punch.

"Goodnight, Alec," I said, outwardly maintaining my composure. I didn't want him to know that I was about to keel over from shock. "Drive safely."

I quickly returned to the house for Marley, my heart beating like a hummingbird's wings.

CHAPTER 12

I WALKED across the open fields to where the Starry Hollow matchball team was playing against a neighboring town. I had no clue what matchball was, but, whatever it was, there was an impressive crowd gathered for a game at the high school level.

I turned to the friendly-looking troll standing next to me. "Do they always draw so many spectators?"

He chuckled. "They do when Jordy Hoskins is on the field. She's Starry Hollow's great hope for the colony championship title this year."

So Jordy truly was a star athlete. I thought Cindy was exaggerating. "Which one is she?"

He pointed to the far end of the field. "Brown ponytail. Moves like a tornado. I've never seen a kid that intense. Then again, consider the source."

I frowned. "The source?"

He pointed again, this time to the edge of the field closest to us. "Check out her dad right there. The guy's a legend. No one's surprised that his daughter is so insanely good. I hear he trains her hard, though." He clucked his tongue. "I wouldn't trade places with Jordy Hoskins for all the trophies in the world."

I watched as Jordy's dad paced the length of the field, gesticulating wildly as she grabbed the ball and zoomed toward the goalposts.

"Her dad was an athlete, too?" I asked.

The troll nodded and I tried not to be distracted by his excessively wide nose. I could lose PP3 in one of his nostrils.

"He led the team to the championships when he was in school," the troll said. "I remember coming to watch him play when my older sister went here. Everyone thought he would go pro."

"But he didn't?" I queried.

"Nope. A knee injury. Happens to a lot of centaurs."

"That's too bad," I said. "What does he do now?"

"Works over at the healer's office as an assistant. I heard he wanted to train as a healer, but he didn't have the grades."

"So healers can be centaurs?" I asked.

The troll looked at me sideways. "Yes," he said slowly. "Why would you think they couldn't? Got a thing about big guys not being capable?"

"Absolutely not," I said quickly. "I just didn't realize it was open to anyone. I thought maybe only certain paranormals could be healers, like druids."

"That's racist," the troll said, and turned his attention back to the field.

Even though I had no inkling what was happening on the field, I could tell Jordy was a natural talent. The combination of innate ability and discipline was sure to serve her well. Somewhere in the distance, bells chimed and the teams retreated to the sidelines for a break. Jordy went straight to her father. He gave her a jubilant fist bump and I could tell from her broad smile that she was happy to have pleased him. For a brief moment, I pictured my own dad and my chest tightened. Although I wasn't an award-winning athlete or an academic scholar, I liked to think I made him proud in my own way. I wondered whether he'd be upset to know I was in Starry Hollow now, after all his efforts to keep me away.

"They seem to have a good relationship," I said, blinking back a tear. *Get a grip, Ember*, I chastised myself. This wasn't *Field of Dreams*. I needed to focus on the task at hand.

The troll nodded emphatically. "Oh, yeah. You don't grow them much closer than Jordy and Bruce. Everyone thought he'd be so disappointed not to have a son to follow in his hoofsteps, but Jordy was a gift from the gods."

"She's an only child?" I asked.

"Yeah. I heard from another parent that Jordy's mom couldn't have any more kids after Jordy. Some kind of complications during the birth."

Ouch. I didn't envy her complicated delivery. My heart went out to any woman who suffered during pregnancy or childbirth. Society acted like it should be the easiest, most natural event in the world, but it really wasn't for a lot of women. I still remembered trying desperately to breastfeed Marley and failing miserably. I'd felt so ashamed, like I wasn't a good mother. At times, I still struggled with feeling like I wasn't good enough for Marley. That she deserved better.

The team enjoyed a brief huddle before returning to the field. I got the impression that I wouldn't be able to talk to Jordy during the game, so I decided to simply watch and see what I could learn.

What I learned was that Jordy had the focus of an Olympian gymnast on the balance beam. She was unstoppable. I wasn't a sports fan, but even I appreciated the skills she possessed. She bobbed, she weaved, and she outsmarted her opponents on the field. I almost felt sorry for her teammates. It was clearly the Jordy Hoskins Show out there and they were used to it.

Out of the corner of my eye, I spotted a young satyr lingering on the sidelines. His necklace of crystals sparkled in the sunlight.

"Is that Spencer?" I asked the troll.

"I don't know his name, but I've seen him with Jordy around town. They run in a little gang." He hesitated. "The dead elf, too. Clover…"

"Grover," I corrected him.

The troll shook his head. "I hope they catch whoever did it soon. Makes you nervous to walk alone at night."

I highly doubted the huge troll worried about walking alone at night, but I thought it would be rude to argue the point.

"I think I'll go say hi," I said. "Nice talking to you." I threaded my way through the onlookers to where Spencer was standing. He seemed to be alone.

He gave me a cursory glance. "You look familiar. Are you Benny's mom?"

"Nope. Benny would not be on my list of favorite names," I said.

His brow wrinkled. "What's wrong with Benny?"

"Nothing," I replied. "It's just not a name for a kid. I guess if it's short for Benjamin…" I shook my head. "Nope. Even then I'd call him Ben or maybe Benji. Benny is a no-go."

Spencer inched away from me.

"You're Spencer, right?" I asked.

Now he *really* wanted to escape. "Yeah. How'd you know?"

"Are you here to watch Jordy play?"

He gave me serious side-eye. "Maybe. Why?"

"Is she your girlfriend?"

He tugged on his necklace. "No, we're just friends."

"How about Grover?" I asked. "Was he involved with Jordy?"

Spencer's hand dropped to his side. "Who are you again?"

"Ember Rose. I write for the local paper and I'm doing a story on Grover. I want to talk about his life and that includes his friends."

Spencer seemed to relax. "Right. No, Jordy and Grover were friends. The four of us grew up together."

"Four?" I queried. "You mean Aldo?"

"Yeah. You talked to him already, didn't you?"

"I did," I replied. "He told you about it?"

Spencer lowered his gaze to the grass. "Of course. It's not every day you talk to the sheriff and a reporter about your dead friend. Kinda newsworthy."

"I hear the four of you had a lot of late nights recently," I said. "Grover was having trouble keeping up in school."

Spencer kicked the dirt with his hoof. "So what? We're teenagers. We're supposed to stay out late."

I dropped my voice. "Are you supposed to do drugs, too?" I caught his guilty expression before he managed to hide it.

"We're not into stuff like that," he said.

"What about your out-of-body experiences?" I asked.

His brow lifted. "How do you know about that? Who's been talking to you? Aldo?"

I shrugged. "I've been investigating Grover's last few weeks. I've heard a lot of things. Maybe you can clarify some of them for me."

Spencer glanced nervously at the field. "I don't think so."

I followed his gaze to where Jordy was high-giving her dad again. "You don't want Jordy to know you've talked to me? Is that it?"

Spencer's jaw tensed. "There's nothing to say."

"Listen, I've had out-of-body experiences," I said quietly. "I know what it's like." Of course, mine was from astral projection, not drugs, but Spencer didn't need to know that.

He seemed surprised. "Yeah? It's cool, right? Like touching the faces of the gods."

My experience involved moving around the woods like a snail without a shell, but, sure, let's go with faces of the gods. "Absolutely. Was Grover into it? I know the experience can freak some paranormals out. Not everyone's cut out for living on the edge."

Spencer appeared to warm to my attitude. "They don't get it. Grover did, though. He was hooked. He..." Spencer stopped abruptly. "Good game, Jordy. Hey, Bruce."

The centaur flared his nostrils. "Spencer. You were supposed to be watching the game to give Jordy feedback on her throwing. That was your one task."

"Sorry," Spencer mumbled. "I got to talking..."

Bruce fixed his attention on me. "Sorry to interrupt, but we take matchball very seriously."

Jordy's hand rested on her hip. "And Spencer's supposed to be helping. Everyone wants this championship."

"I saw most of it," Spencer said. "We only talked for a couple of minutes."

I thrust out my hand and shook the centaur's. "Ember Rose. Nice to meet you both. Great game, Jordy. You have amazing skills."

Bruce ruffled his daughter's hair. "She sure does. Just like her old man."

She swatted his hand away. "It isn't all genetic, you know. I work hard."

"Because I make you work hard," Bruce said. "Gotta keep up the pressure."

"Sounds too intense for me," I said. "I'm more about the Jacuzzi bath afterward."

I seemed to shrink two sizes in Bruce's eyes. "That's paranormal nature," he said. "Nobody wants to push the envelope. It's all about the easy road these days."

Sheesh. I was suddenly grateful for my father's relaxed approach to life. Jordy was liable to burn out before her twenty-first birthday.

"I don't know about here, but, in the human world, stress is a real killer," I told them. "There's something to be said for chilling out."

"I'll chill out when I'm dead," Jordy said, and her brown eyes rounded. "I didn't mean that." Her hand flew to cover her mouth.

Bruce patted her shoulder. "We're all still at a loss over Grover. That's why concentrating on matchball is so important. It gives you something to focus on."

"My counselor says I can use it as a coping device," Jordy said.

"That's smart," I replied. "What about you, Spencer? How have you been coping?"

Spencer seemed to be at a loss for words. "I meditate," he finally said. "I take a yoga class with Iris."

"The coven's High Priestess?" I queried.

Spencer snapped his fingers. "That's her. Nice lady. She's got a real calming presence."

"If you were any calmer, you'd be asleep," Bruce said, and Spencer's face reddened.

I could tell I wouldn't get any more information out of Spencer or Jordy with a parental figure around. I decided to cut my losses.

"It was great to meet you," I said. "Good luck with the championships."

"Thank you," Jordy said. "I want to win so I can dedicate the trophy to Grover. He used to come to all my games."

"That's sweet," I said. "I bet he would've liked that."

"He was easy to please," Jordy said. "Never objected to anything."

"Come on, Jordy," her father said. "We need to get back to the team." He crooked a finger at Spencer. "You too, boy. Time to make yourself useful."

Spencer hurried after the father-daughter dynamic duo. I'd need to do a little digging on the group's out-of-body experiences. Then again, since there weren't any drugs identified in the dead elf's system, his death couldn't have been the result of an overdose. Nobody took wolfsbane or nightshade to get high.

As I left the field, my thoughts shifted to my dad. He never wanted me to be the 'best' at anything. He only wanted me to be the best version of me. I realized that it was exactly the way I felt about Marley. Although she was smarter and more capable than most kids her age, I didn't feel the need to push her in any given direction. She'd find her own path, just as I found mine...Okay, maybe I was still finding mine, but, I had to admit, finding it was half the fun.

Thirty minutes later, I found myself face-to-face with my own intense coach in the woods behind Rose Cottage. Marigold marched in front of me, hands clasped behind her back like the cheerleader-cum-drill sergeant she aspired to be. "You've been doing very well with astral projection. Therefore, I propose we take a break from it and explore another skill."

I'd recently learned to separate my consciousness from my body and essentially have it walk around like a ghost. I had to admit, it was one of the coolest things I'd learned to do as a witch. I kept waiting for the right opportunity to freak out Marley, but she'd made such strides with her anxiety, I refused to be the one to set her back for the sake of a joke.

I placed my hands on my hips. "Are you tired of my astral projecting already?"

"Am I tired of watching you jump out from behind a tree and say 'boo'?" Marigold gave a mock laugh. "Don't be ridiculous. I treasure those moments with you."

"Now you're being grumpy," I accused.

"Not at all," she replied. "Why don't we continue with telekinesis today? You can try to lift something heavier than a branch. Exercise those psychic muscles."

I rubbed my palms together. "I'm down with that." Telekinesis was also a pretty amazing psychic skill. Who wouldn't want to move objects just by thinking about them? I was living the dream.

"Should we start small again and work our way up?" Marigold proposed.

"Do I look like an amateur to you?"

Marigold folded her arms. "Very much so, as a matter fact."

"Fine," I huffed. "I'll start with that twig over there." I pointed to an anemic twig at the base of a live oak tree. I focused my will and tried to lift the twig into the air.

"You're doing that weird thing with your eyes again," Marigold said.

My concentration broke and I glared at my instructor. "I do *not* do weird things with my eyes."

"That's because you can't see yourself," Marigold replied smoothly. "I'll try to record you one of these days so you can see how absurd you look."

Her comment reminded me of Thomas's desire to capture his likeness while asleep. "Did you see the sand sculptures?"

"Of course," Marigold replied. "Florian was in charge. I

believe the entire coven was threatened with bodily harm if we didn't show our support."

I must've missed that memo. "You know Marley and I found the dead body in the sand casket, right?"

"Naturally," Marigold replied. "News like that travels at the speed of light. How is Marley?"

"She's okay," I said. "I managed to shield her from it. It was a creepy moment, though. It's been haunting me, that's for sure."

"And the investigation is ongoing?"

"It is." I paused. "Can you think of any reason why paranormals would use vampire blood aside from trying to turn someone?"

Marigold inspected me. "Why? What are you into?"

"Into?" I echoed. "Nothing. What do you mean?"

She narrowed her eyes. "I don't tolerate drugs in my classroom."

I surveyed the woods. "This isn't your classroom."

"Anywhere I happen to be teaching qualifies as my classroom."

"Can vampire blood give you an out-of-body experience?" I asked. "I mean, does it ever behave like a drug in someone's system?"

"You're asking because of the elf?" she asked. When I nodded, she visibly relaxed. "I've never heard of vampire blood doing that. I know once someone is turned, all of their senses become heightened, but that's not from the blood alone."

I frowned. "Right."

"And vampire blood also has healing properties, don't forget."

"I know. Is it true the blood can only heal certain ailments?" I pressed. "It's not a cure for everything, right?

Like, if he had cancer, nobody would suggest vampire blood to cure it."

"Of course not," Marigold said. "Why do you ask? Did the Maitland boy have cancer?"

"No, no. He wasn't ill, although the autopsy report also showed traces of nightshade and wolfsbane, so I guess that would make someone pretty sick."

Marigold blinked. "*Two* deadly poisons?"

"I know, as though one wasn't enough." I blew out a breath in frustration. "What if he was accidentally exposed to the poisons when he found them in the ceramic gnome and then someone tried to use vampire blood to heal him?" But then why hide it? Why not rush him to the healer's and explain what happened?

"So you're looking for either a vampire or someone with access to vampire blood," Marigold said.

I tapped my cheek. "Possibly. Keep it under your witch hat, though," I said. "The sheriff wants it to fly under the radar as much as possible while we investigate."

"*We* investigate?" Marigold repeated. "What about Deputy Bolan?"

"That leprechaun already hates me," I said. "What's one more reason?"

Marigold eyed me curiously. "Why are you acting as the sheriff's right hand? Is it because you want more than his hand?"

I glared at her. "I'm not his right hand. I represent *Vox Populi*. It's my aunt's newspaper, remember?"

"And that means you and the sheriff are joined at the hip now?" Marigold asked. "Can't you investigate separately from him?"

"I can and often do," I said, bristling.

"How does Alec Hale feel about all this time with the sheriff?" Marigold asked.

I groaned. "Take your fishing pole and go home, Marigold. I'm not telling you anything except that Alec is very much in favor of keeping the relationship professional." His recent kiss notwithstanding, of course. I still wasn't sure what prompted it. Too much bucksberry fizz at dinner was my guess.

"Like the sheriff, I'm sure," Marigold said, in a tone that suggested the exact opposite.

I focused my will on a nearby leaf and raised it off the ground until it was in front of her cheek, then I used it to gently slap her.

"A leaf," Marigold said. "How clever. It felt like being kissed by the wind."

"That wasn't my intent." The leaf drifted back to the ground.

"Does the sheriff know the source of the wolfsbane and nightshade?" Marigold asked.

"Not yet. I know he checked with the schools and the coven and no supplies were missing." When I investigated the death of Fleur, the Maiden, I discovered that the schools kept certain poisons on hand for academic purposes, but they were almost impossible steal.

"Well, I think it's very sweet that you've trusted me with insider info from your boyfriend," Marigold said. "If I hear anything useful, I'll be sure to pass it along."

"The sheriff is *not* my boyfriend," I snapped.

"Have you been on a date with him?" she asked.

I dug the toe of my shoe in the dirt. "I've been out with him. I don't know if it constitutes a date."

"Have you kissed him?" she asked.

I glared at her. "Now you're just being nosy!"

Marigold laughed. "So I am. If you're not going to share, then let's get back to work, shall we? These acorns aren't going to raise themselves."

CHAPTER 13

I stood in the grocery section of the Wish Market, clutching a wicker basket. I knew I only needed to imagine a slug parfait in order to have one materialize in my basket. The problem was that my mind didn't seem to want to cooperate. The image was sure to be disgusting, so my brain insisted on staging a rebellion.

"Come on, wimp," I scolded myself. "I promised my familiar."

In the next aisle over, I heard someone mention the name 'Jordy.' How many Jordys could there be in Starry Hollow? I poked my head around the corner to see a lithe nymph with a basket full of food. I waited until she put her phone away to intrude.

"Excuse me," I said. "Are you Mrs. Hoskins?"

The older nymph gave me a curious look. "I am."

I gave her my friendliest smile and hoped it didn't come across as psychotic. "I met Jordy and your husband recently."

"Then you were either at one of her games or the fields where they practice," Mrs. Hoskins said. "Those are basically the two places they're together outside of the house."

"It was at one of her games," I said. "She's an amazing talent."

"She really is," Mrs. Hoskins said. "She has her father to thank for it. He was determined to shape her into an athlete from the moment she was born."

"You didn't object?" I asked. "Maybe you wanted to steer her in another direction?"

"There's no stopping Bruce when he wants something," she said. "He's a force to be reckoned with."

Hmm. Her tone suggested that maybe she minded after all. "You weren't much of an athlete, I take it? Me neither. I trip over my own feet." Or a ceramic garden gnome. Take your pick.

"I'm not a clumsy giant," she said, "but I'd rather make something with my hands. I'm more of a creative type. That's why I was so pleased when Jordy got an after school job at the ceramics place."

I balked. "Sierra's Ceramics?"

Mrs. Hoskins smiled. "Yes. Do you know it?"

"I do. I understand Sierra runs a tight ship."

"Absolutely," the nymph agreed. "It's been ideal for us. Between athletics and school and work, there's no time for Jordy to find trouble." Her expression darkened. "Maybe things would have been different for Grover if he'd been as busy as our Jordy."

"She's an All-Star, right?" I asked.

Her mother beamed. "She was last year, so we're hoping for it again this year. Bruce is determined to make sure she gets noticed by a university scout."

"Would that mean a scholarship?" I asked. I knew it was likely in the human world, but I wasn't sure about the paranormal one.

"Oh, yes," she said. "And it would make a huge difference

to our finances. We wouldn't need to choose between retirement and our daughter's education."

Yep, just like the human world.

"When does Jordy work at Sierra's?" And how did she possibly have time to fit it all in? I thought I was reasonably organized and efficient, but Jordy put me to shame. I had to find a way to fit in exercise soon, so I could lose the 'troll roll' I developed around my midsection thanks to those excessive Sunday dinners.

"She works weekends there," her mother said. "We limited her to weekends so as not to interfere with her school or athletic schedule. If I had my way, she wouldn't work at all, but her father insisted. He thinks establishing a work ethic at a young age is important and he knew Sierra would be a real taskmaster."

"He knows Sierra?" I inquired.

"Oh, yes," Mrs. Hoskins said. "They've been friends for years. Sierra's not exactly my brand of brew, but you can't argue with her success."

"Sounds like Jordy is destined for success, too," I said. And I suddenly felt painfully inadequate as a mother.

"I hope so because I want her to get to choose the life she wants," her mother said. "But, honestly, I worry a job adds stress that she doesn't need. Plenty of time for stress when you're older."

"So true," I replied. "Speaking of which, what are your thoughts on Grover? Is there a chance he was into something he shouldn't have been in order to ease stress?" Something that resulted in out-of-body experiences? "He seemed to be struggling with schoolwork in recent weeks."

Mrs. Hoskins pressed her hand to her mouth in an effort to stifle a cry. "That poor family. Every time I think about it, I want to dissolve. I can't imagine what they're going through.

I reached out to them, but they seem to want to keep to themselves right now."

"Are you close with them?" I asked.

"Not really," she replied. "They're nice enough, but the kids are pretty independent. It isn't like when they're little and you need to befriend the parents. And the Maitlands always seem so busy with their jobs. I'd say Bruce spent more time with Grover than his parents did. He loves hanging out with Jordy and her friends." She gave a tolerant smile. "Takes him back to his glory days, I suspect."

I silently agreed. I got the impression from the game that Bruce was living vicariously through his daughter.

"How would you characterize Jordy's relationship with Grover?" I asked. "Any romance there?"

Mrs. Hoskins gave a dismissive wave of her hand. "Who can tell with teenagers? If there was anything romantic between them, she'd never let on. Not to me anyway. Maybe to her dad, although he's never mentioned it. That group is so tight, it's hard to tell."

I felt a pang of envy. I would have liked a group of friends like that in high school, so loyal and tight-knit. My father discouraged close friendships with others, which I used to resent. Now that I'd discovered my true heritage, however, I understood that he was trying to protect me.

"How does Jordy seem to be coping with Grover's death?" I asked.

"Definitely sad, as you'd expect," she said. "I've had a hard time getting her out of bed in the morning, which is usually not a problem for us. Jordy always takes care of herself, but there's definitely been a backslide in maturity. She hasn't been eating as much either. Her father commented on it last night, which is why I'm here now." She held up the basket. "Buying her favorite foods. Bruce threatened to take away her phone if she didn't eat."

Yikes. Talk about control issues.

"Does she see anyone at school? Maybe a grief counselor?" I asked.

"I know she's talked to Mrs. Bass—that's her counselor at school. I wish she would talk to us, but you know you can't force a conversation with a teenager. You may as well try to force a shark to walk on land."

"I appreciate your time, Mrs. Hoskins," I said. "I think as long as you keep letting Jordy know you're available to talk, that's the best you can do." That was what I tried to do with Marley, although at this point I had no trouble getting Marley to talk. It was the teenage years I worried about, though. Marley could easily become Jordy if I didn't stay vigilant.

"That's the plan," she replied. "It was nice chatting with you." The nymph turned her attention back to the shelves of exotic foods and I made a beeline for the exit. The slug parfait would have to wait. I couldn't even pretend to be sad about it.

Sierra's Ceramics was a factory-style building, located in the northwest section of town. Before I managed to reach the main entrance, two trolls approached me. They wore matching blue uniforms with silver badges. Rent-a-Troll.

"This is private property," the troll on the left snarled. "You should head back out to the main road, then make a left if you want to go into town."

I shook my head. "No, I'm in the right place. I'm here to see Sierra."

"Do you have an appointment?" the second troll asked. "I don't have anyone on the schedule."

"This lady works for the newspaper. You should let her through." The mumbling voice was oddly familiar.

"Hello, Aldo," I said, as the druid appeared beside me. "Do you work here, too?"

He shook the shaggy hair from his eyes. "Yeah, after school and on Saturdays. Are you here because of your story on Grover?"

"Yes," I said, and suddenly remembered Lotus's comment about Grover getting a part-time job when school started. Duh. Of course he worked with his friends. That also explained the Mother's Day gifts.

Aldo fixed his attention on the trolls. "Let us through, guys. Sierra will want to talk to her."

To my amazement, one of the trolls deactivated the ward and they stepped aside for us to pass.

Once we were inside, I turned to Aldo. "Thanks. I thought they were going to chase me back to my car."

He offered a shy smile. "They're harmless. I've been working here for over a year, so I know them pretty well. Sierra hired them after an incident with a stalker. Some goblin from a dating site tracked her down here. She's been a little paranoid ever since."

Who could blame her? It wasn't easy being a single woman in any town, paranormal or human.

Aldo led me down a long, narrow corridor to a lonely office tucked away from the rest of the rooms. He pressed his palm flat against the door and said his name. The door clicked open. My attention was drawn straight to a large woman sitting on an exercise ball. She wore a headset and seemed to be in mid-conversation. She held up a cautionary finger when she saw us.

"Absolutely not, Edgar," Sierra snapped. "The waybill says the fourteenth, so that's when I expect delivery." She paused to listen. "Since when do I give a flying unicorn about sick children? I have a business to run here. I don't need excuses. I need results." She flicked off the headset and tossed it aside with a groan of disgust. "I don't know what ever happened to the sanctity of agreements. Everyone seems to want the world to cater to their problems." She seemed to register my presence for the first time. "Who are you?"

I stepped forward. "Ember Rose. I'm a reporter for *Vox Populi*."

Sierra glanced sharply at Aldo. "Why in Odin's name are you escorting a reporter through my building? Have you had a brain aneurysm that your uncle couldn't cure?"

"He didn't know I was coming," I said, feeling the need to defend the young druid. "We happened to meet at the entrance. I was hoping to talk to you about Grover Maitland."

Sierra rolled the ball forward with her bottom and busied herself at her desk. "Great kid. Tragic death. What do you want to know?"

Phew, and I thought I was tough. I looked at Aldo over my shoulder. "For one thing, I didn't realize you hired so many teenagers from school."

"Not all of us work the same shifts," Aldo said. "And only my crew works on Saturdays."

Sierra silenced him with a harsh look that did not escape my attention.

"Aldo, why don't you get to work and leave me with Miss Rose?" Sierra said, adopting a sweeter tone.

"Sure," he said. He seemed to realize that he might have stepped out of line. "I'll even do some painting." He smiled at me. "Sierra knows how much I hate painting."

"What's to hate?" Sierra snapped. "We use magic here. It's not like it's labor intensive."

His face reddened and he backtracked out of the office, mumbling a quick goodbye before disappearing into the corridor.

"It can't be easy, dealing with teenagers every day," I said. "I have a hard time understanding them. Makes me feel old."

"I'm sorry if I seemed to be silencing him," she said. "Between you and me, I pay these kids under the table, so I try not to draw attention to the fact that they work here. I want these kids to save their money, not pay taxes on it."

"And I suppose your business saves money, too." Because Sierra made it perfectly clear a moment ago that she didn't give a flying unicorn about kids, sick or otherwise.

Sierra eyed me with a laser focus. "Stop giving off that judgmental vibe. You can't tell me the coven doesn't cut corners to save a few coins."

"I'm not privy to the coven's finances," I replied. "How did you know I was a witch?"

"Because I'm not a moron," Sierra shot back. "Valkyries can sniff out a witch a mile away. One of our many gifts."

So she was a valkyrie. Glad I didn't need to ask. I got the sense she'd be offended by my ignorance.

"And I hear a head for business is one of your other gifts," I said.

"Valkyries have a certain reputation to uphold," she conceded.

"And what reputation is that?"

"Fierce," she replied. "Whether that's in war or business. There's no war raging at the moment, so I choose to use my skills in business."

"So tell me about Grover. Was he any trouble?"

"Never once," Sierra replied.

"And the others? Are they any trouble?"

Sierra snorted. "Look at me, Miss Rose. Do you think for one second those kids would be trouble for me?"

Nope. Not a chance. "Have to ask," I said with an apologetic smile.

"They're all good, hardworking kids," Sierra said. "I

wouldn't hire any losers. It's not my style. This is a business, not a charity."

How could I ask about the bags of deadly plants that Aunt Hyacinth's spell revealed? I didn't want the valkyrie to pummel me with that exercise ball. On the other hand, I couldn't let some Norse warrior intimidate me. I had my Jersey pride to consider. I swallowed my apprehension and plowed ahead.

"Have you ever caught any of the teenagers with drugs or any type of illegal substance?" I asked.

Sierra's eyes widened. "On my property? I'd never jeopardize the company like that. I've put too much time and energy building this into a successful business."

I decided to keep pushing. "Do you have any knowledge of their involvement with illegal substances outside of work hours?"

Sierra gave me an appraising look. "No, I have no knowledge of that. They're an intense bunch, that's for sure, especially Jordy Hoskins, but they're good kids."

"And you're friends with Jordy's dad, right?"

She snorted again. "That's why I understand her intensity. Her dad is wired exactly the same way. He can be a challenging paranormal to deal with."

Wow. There was the cauldron calling the kettle black, as Hazel liked to say.

"You don't think he pushes her too hard?" I asked.

Sierra shrugged. "Not my meadow. Not my unicorn."

Right. "Thanks for talking to me."

"Sure thing. Next time, though, make an appointment or I'll have my trolls toss you out. Reporter or not, I take trespassing very seriously here. I'm sure you don't want the sheriff coming down hard on you."

My throat tightened. Didn't I?

"I'll keep that in mind," I said.

Sierra hit a buzzer. "Wait here and my trolls will escort you out. Wouldn't want you getting lost."

Or something else getting found.

As I left quietly nestled between the Rent-a-Trolls, I had no doubt I hadn't seen the last of Sierra's Ceramics. I wasn't sure what the connection was, but I was determined to find out.

CHAPTER 14

IN THE OFFICE the next day, the first thing I noticed about my vampire boss was the absence of his usual three-piece suit. Alec was always impeccably dressed, but today he wore jeans and a formfitting black T-shirt. He looked like a walking advertisement for procreation. He may as well have worn a shirt with a skull and crossbones and the words 'jump my bones' emblazoned across the front. Even his hair was in casual mode. Instead of slicked-back blond locks, he went product-free and let his natural waves tousle, or whatever waves did.

"Are you on an undercover assignment?" Tanya asked. The fairy office manager gaped at Alec like she'd never seen him before. Not that I blamed her. I was fairly certain I was gaping, too. Even Bentley seemed floored.

"No, I leave the undercover assignments to the sheriff's office." Alec chuckled and I noticed a dimple flash in his left cheek. Since when did Alec have a dimple? Then it hit me. The dimple wasn't new. It was the extent of the smile that was new.

"You look great, boss," Bentley said. "Very casual."

Alec patted Bentley's cheek. "There's a good lad. Such a great attitude."

Bentley beamed and the tips of his pointed ears burned crimson. "You were both out yesterday. Tanya and I thought maybe you came down with food poisoning at the Sunday dinner."

"I meant to come in, but I got sidetracked," I said. "I'm going to type up my notes now."

"I got sidetracked, too," Alec said. "I stayed in my pajamas the whole day and watched movies."

Bentley laughed, assuming it was a joke, but Alec's expression didn't change.

"Thank you for reminding me about the wonderful Sunday dinner, Bentley," Alec said, and offered me a peck on the cheek. "Ember, your aunt is a perfect hostess. I had such a lovely time. Not that I expected anything less."

"Ember?" I repeated, touching the spot on my cheek where his lips had just been.

Alec grinned. "That's your name, isn't it?"

"Yes, but you always call me Miss Rose."

"Miss Rose is so formal, wouldn't you agree?" he said. "Ember is more fetching. A spark. A glow. It suits you."

My name was fetching? "Technically, it's more like a dying fire than a glow." I placed a hand on his forehead to test for a fever. Cool as...an undead guy. "Are you feeling okay?"

"I feel marvelous," he said. "Why do you ask?" His tone was so unexpectedly chipper, I had to take a step back.

"Um, no reason." I stood there awkwardly, not sure how to talk to this relaxed version of Alec Hale. I exchanged a furtive glance with Bentley, who seemed equally confused.

"You should join me in my office," Alec told me. "There's something I'd like to share with you."

Now he wanted to share with me? He clasped my hand

and guided me toward his office. I looked helplessly over my shoulder at Tanya and Bentley, with their matching unhinged jaws.

He closed the door behind us and trotted over to his desk with a spring in his step I'd never seen before.

"Should I sit here?" I asked.

"No, no," he replied. "Come sit at my desk. I want to show you something on the computer I've been working on. I'm super excited about this project."

My eyes bulged. "You're…super excited about something?" I'd never heard Alec use the word 'super' to describe anything. Not even Superman.

He patted the edge of his chair. "You're small. You can squeeze beside me."

I certainly wasn't about to reject the opportunity to sit close to that tight butt. I dropped down beside him and looked at the screen, immediately recognizing the title of the document. It was *Filthy Witch*, a work-in-progress I'd spotted on here when Alec was incapacitated by an infectious disease.

"I've finished a draft of my new book," he said. "I thought you should know it was inspired by you."

I balked. "By me?" And he was admitting it? Was this the same Alec Hale who called me Miss Rose in order to maintain emotional distance from me? Surely not.

He nodded. "I typically write these long fantasy books, but I thought it would be fun to mix things up a little. This story is bursting with romance. I think I'll publish it under a pen name. A.B. Ellis."

I struggled to speak. "Are you sure it was inspired by me?"

Alec grinned, his fangs on full display. "Naturally. Who else has captured my fancy so completely? I haven't felt this alive since I was…alive."

I shifted in the seat. I was unaccustomed to Alec being so

forward. The vampire was all about restraint and decorum. "I thought you didn't want to…I thought because of my aunt…"

He leaned closer to me, his breath hot on my neck. "I want to, Ember. Make no mistake. Very much."

I shivered. "Are you showing this to me because you want me to read it?"

"I would love that. Of course, I'll completely understand if you're too busy," he said. "You're a force of nature, Ember. I know you have a lot in your cauldron with magic training, your work here, and your delightful daughter."

"Oh, I'll make time to read this," I said.

"Perfect, I'll email you a copy." He attached the document to my email address and hit send. "I can't wait to know what you think of it. It's definitely a divergence from my usual style."

"Yes, it certainly is," I said, unabashedly staring at him. Sweet baby Elvis. His face was unbelievably gorgeous. I couldn't imagine how many women he'd seduced with those sensual lips alone. I felt the bulge of his bicep as his arm brushed against mine and I instinctively pulled away.

"Ember, would you like to have dinner with me tonight?" he asked softly.

The question was so unexpected, I nearly burst into inappropriate laughter. "Dinner in public? Are you sure?"

"Of course I'm certain," he replied. "There's no one in Starry Hollow I'd rather share a meal with."

"Okay," I said. My stomach felt like a hive full of swarming bees. "Let me make arrangements for Marley."

"Next time we'll include her," he said.

Next time? "You want Marley to come to dinner with us?"

"Your daughter's company is highly enjoyable," Alec said. "I look forward to spending more time with her. With both of you."

This had to be because of Sheriff Nash. Alec must've heard about my recent outings with the werewolf and decided to take action.

"Marley would love that," I said.

"You seem surprised that I like her," Alec said. "Whatever have I done to give you the impression that your daughter was less than adequate in my eyes?"

"Nothing," I stammered. "You've always been good to Marley." I couldn't bring myself to mention his odd behavior. Part of me feared he'd revert to his normal standoffish self.

He grinned again, flashing that previously hidden dimple. "I'll pick you up at eight. Does that suit you?"

"It suits me fine," I said.

"Excellent," he said. "I look forward to it."

I had no idea who the vampire was sitting next to me, but I knew one thing—I couldn't wait to go out with him tonight.

Alec's driver arrived promptly at eight o'clock. I did a final inspection in the mirror before hustling downstairs. No bra straps showing—check. Tummy control—check. Tasteful cleavage rather than tasty—um, I'd need to fix that. I was careful not to wear red, so as not to send Alec into full vampire mode. I had no desire to bring out the fanged beast in him, not tonight anyway.

As I passed by the hall bathroom, Marley poked her head through the doorway with a mouth full of toothpaste.

"Ewe like booful," she said.

"Thank you, sweetheart," I said. "You look beautiful, too. Now go rinse."

I said goodbye to Mrs. Babcock, who sat in front of the fireplace knitting a blanket. "I'll do a bit of knitting with Marley before bed, if you don't mind."

"As long as she's not up too late," I said.

PP3 tried to follow me out the door, walking so close to my feet that I nearly tripped over him.

"You've got to stay here, buddy," I said, opening the front door. "This is a nice place. No dogs allowed."

How about raccoons? Raoul stood in the shadows, near the pink rose bushes.

"Why are you lurking in my front garden?" I demanded.

Because you don't invite me in, he said.

On the other side of the door, PP3 growled. I jabbed a finger in the direction of the door.

"*That's* why I don't invite you in," I said. "PP3 is old and set in his ways. He's not going to embrace a raccoon with open arms."

I should hope not, Raoul said. *That would be weird. Dude's a dog.*

I rolled my eyes. "I need to go, Raoul. Try not to get into any trouble."

The back window of the car slid down. "Ember? Is there an issue?"

"No, it's fine." I hurried to the car as the driver opened the door for me. "Thank you."

I scooted in beside Alec and inhaled his familiar scent. Evergreen and musk. *Sweet baby Elvis*, he smelled divine.

"Ahem, Ember." He tapped the side of his head.

I cringed. "Crap on a stick, sorry."

He smiled. "Don't be sorry. I enjoy knowing how divine I smell. I just wanted to warn you before your thoughts turned in another direction."

I closed my eyes and concentrated on cloaking my thoughts. It wasn't difficult, but I managed to let my guard down around Alec more than I should.

"You look as divine as I smell," he said, his gaze lingering on me long enough to make my pulse quicken.

"Thank you," I said. "I credit my DNA, something I had absolutely no hand in."

Alec's sensual lips quirked and his hand moved to cover mine. "This is guaranteed to be a splendid evening."

From his incredible lips to the gods' ears.

When we walked into the restaurant, heads actually swiveled. I quickly realized they were gawking at Alec's new look, rather than at us dining together. It was like Black Leather Sandy from *Grease* showing up for swordfish and risotto when everyone was expecting Uptight Ponytail Sandy.

Ever the gentleman, he pulled out my chair before he sat and opened his menu. I considered myself a feminist, but I also liked when someone pulled out my chair, held open a door for me, and cooked and cleaned for me. Hmm. Maybe I was just lazy.

"Excellent. My favorite dessert is a special tonight," he said.

"Which one is that?" I scanned the choices on my menu. My eyes were drawn to the word 'chocolate' wherever it appeared on the menu. Typical.

He gazed at me over the top of his menu. "See if you can guess."

I studied the dessert options. Blood red velvet cake seemed too obvious. Magical Mud Pie didn't grab me. There was one traditionally human dessert listed.

"Crème brûlée?" I queried.

He set down the menu. "That's right. How did you know?"

"Process of elimination," I said. "Why a human world dessert?" Especially when Starry Hollow offered such amazing food.

"The first time I tasted crème brûlée, I was in Paris," he said. "I thought I'd never tasted anything so delicious in all my years as a vampire. I vowed to order it whenever I was fortunate enough to see it on a menu."

"Tonight's your lucky night then," I said.

He winked at me. "I sure hope so."

My neck warmed. Part of me felt guilty for enjoying our flirtation so much, especially because of Sheriff Nash. I wasn't used to having any males in my life since Karl died, let alone two. I was out of my depth.

"How would you feel about karaoke after dinner?" Alec asked.

I nearly choked on my wine. "I'm sorry. Did you say karaoke? As in singing to a room full of drunk people?"

"Drunk paranormals, but yes," he said. "Being loud and acceptably obnoxious seems right up your alley, no?"

I couldn't even pretend to be offended. "Yes, it does!"

We enjoyed a fabulous dish called lobster akasha and drank an entire bottle of red wine before sharing the crème brûlée.

"I'm surprised you're willing to share," I said. Out of deeply ingrained habit, I used my own spoon.

"With you? Why wouldn't I?" he asked. "If I'm willing to swap bodily fluids with you, I should be willing to split a dessert."

At the mention of bodily fluids, a spoonful of crème brûlée got stuck in my throat. I forced it down and gaped at him. "What bodily fluids?"

He laughed. "Relax, Ember. I meant kissing. When did you become such a prude?"

My mouth dropped open. "I'm not. I just…" I didn't know what to say.

"You do remember that we've kissed, don't you?" He wore a vague smile. "It's a good memory for a chilly night."

"Why are you being so open with me?" I blurted. "What

happened to buttoned-up Alec, the vampire with damaging emotional issues?"

Alec cocked an eyebrow. "Why? Would you like him back?"

I considered the question. "Maybe? There's obviously something appealing about him. About you."

"But you prefer this Alec?"

"I like being able to speak my mind," I said.

"I daresay you have no issue with that—whether I'm in a suit or jeans, makes no difference."

I polished off the last of my drink. To say I was pleasantly buzzed was an understatement. "There are so many times I have to bite my tongue, though. You have no idea."

He leaned forward and gazed at me with such intensity, my insides quivered. "Then bite away, Ember. I think we'd both enjoy it."

Dear Goddess of the Moon. I was about to melt into my chair. Maybe that was what really happened to the Wicked Witch of the West in the *Wizard of Oz*. Dorothy didn't throw a bucket of water. The old witch had some hot vampire flirting madly with her and that was the end of her.

One scoop of crème brûlée remained in the dish. "You go ahead," I said.

"No," he said. "I'd like to watch you eat it."

I held the spoon in mid-air. "You want to watch me eat the last of bit of your favorite dessert?"

He nodded, those kissable lips curving into a sexy smile. "Feel free to make pleasurable noises. You've done it with every other spoonful."

My face turned crimson. "I have?" It didn't surprise me. I was very oral...or vocal.

"Our attraction is undeniable. Wouldn't you agree?"

I swallowed the last bite, very conscious of his eyes on me. "I thought we were supposed to deny it."

He paid the bill before I had a chance to draw breath. "I'm feeling very free at the moment, Ember. Life's too short to ignore a connection like ours."

"Your life isn't short," I said. "You're immortal."

He grinned. "Details." He pushed back his chair and extended a hand. "Shall we?"

"We're seriously going to karaoke?"

"I already know what I'm going to sing," he replied. "Trust me. You're going to love it."

CHAPTER 15

STRANGE BREW WAS the closest place I'd seen to a dive bar in Starry Hollow. It wasn't trendy and upscale like Elixir. Instead, it reminded me of the nameless bars in the Philadelphia metropolitan area. Places where the smoke stuck to you like cobwebs and you needed to wash your clothes twice to get rid of the stench. There was a jukebox tucked away in the corner, and a dryad behind the bar that looked like he was rooted to the floor, which, as a tree nymph, maybe he was.

"Hey, Hank," Alec greeted him.

Hank glanced up from the tap in disbelief. He clearly wasn't used to being greeted by Alec in such a cheerful manner. I couldn't believe Alec voluntarily stepped foot in a place like this.

Alec nudged me. "What would you like to try this evening, Ember? Anything catch your fancy? Aside from me, that is."

My breathing hitched. I was still baffled by this forthright and upbeat version of Alec. It was as though Eeyore had been body snatched by Tigger.

"From the vibe of this place, I'd say we are strictly in ale territory," I said. In my experience, dive bars were generally not the right venue to sample a new cocktail.

Alec chuckled. "I suppose you're right. Hank, we'd like two zazzlewick ales, please."

Hank gave him a thumbs up and set to work. "You realize it's karaoke night, don't you?"

Alec nodded. "Yes, I'm aware of the schedule."

Hank scrunched his nose and stared at the vampire. "But you hate karaoke night. You told me to remind you the next time you wandered in here that it was karaoke so you could leave."

Alec shrugged. "It's a gentleman's prerogative to change his mind."

Hank slid the ales across the counter to us. "Fair enough. You don't strike me as the sort of vampire to do the complete opposite of what you said, though. You usually stick to your word."

My hand froze on the glass. The complete opposite? I squeezed my eyes closed in frustration. I was such an idiot! How did I not realize that Alec's behavior was due to my spell on Wyatt? I must've accidentally zapped Alec when the cat knocked my wand. I'd ignored the obvious because, subconsciously, I wanted to experience this version of Alec. Willful blindness.

"Is something wrong, Ember?" Alec asked with concern.

I didn't know what to say. I certainly wasn't about to admit that I'd inadvertently hexed him into being a better version of himself. On the other hand, it was so nice to spend time with this vampire. I was loath to give it up.

"Everything is great," I said. Or, at least it would be for the remainder of the night. After that, I'd need to reverse the spell. As tempted as I was, I couldn't leave Alec in this state indefinitely. It wasn't fair.

A burst of noise from the entrance drew our attention. My head swiveled and I was shocked to see Sheriff Nash swagger in with Wyatt and Linnea. They seemed shocked to see us.

"Ember, what in Mother Nature's name are you doing here?" Linnea asked.

I inclined my head toward Wyatt. "I should stay the same to you," I replied. "You're here with Wyatt?"

Linnea smiled, drowning us all in Rose-Muldoon beauty. They were a striking family, and the eldest sibling was no exception. I tried not to think of my own tangled dark hair. It served no purpose to want the sleek, white-blond hair I could never have.

"Wyatt knows how much I like to sing," Linnea said. "He suggested we come here tonight so I could show off my pipes."

"I didn't realize you could sing," I said. Not that I was surprised. My cousins seemed blessed with every possible talent. I could understand why residents were both resentful and in awe of them at the same time.

Linnea glanced around the half empty bar. "I'm relieved it isn't crowded. It's been quite some time since I sang in public. I don't want to embarrass myself."

"I think you'd have to work pretty hard to embarrass yourself," I told her. I took a long sip of ale. "Can I get you anything?"

Wyatt appeared between us holding two glasses of ale. "I've got it covered, babe. Don't you worry." He slapped Alec's back. "Good to see you again, sir. That was a great dinner on Sunday, wasn't it?"

Sheriff Nash approached us cautiously. "You were both at Sunday dinner at Thornhold?" His gaze darted from Alec to me.

Linnea gave a dismissive flick of her elegant fingers.

"Mother likes to mix things up every once in a while. I'd asked for Wyatt to be included for the sake of the children, and Mother thought it would be nice to have Alec. After all, he is her favorite employee."

Sheriff Nash grinned. "Employee," he repeated. "Now there's a word I don't have to hear very often. That's the good thing about being the sheriff."

Uh oh. The macho muscles were flexing. This night could go sideways if I wasn't careful.

"Technically, *you* are an employee of Starry Hollow," Alec said. "If you want to be very technical, you work for all of us."

Sheriff Nash scowled. "Well, I don't have to answer to all of you. I operate independently."

"As do I," Alec said. "Need I remind you that I'm a best-selling author. *Vox Populi* is a labor of love rather than a necessity. Can you say the same?"

"Who's ready for another drink?" I interjected. At this point, I wouldn't be surprised if one of them peed a circle around me.

Hank appeared in front of us, as though summoned by the word 'drink.' "I'll pull a few more pints, then I need to get the karaoke started."

"My gorgeous and talented ex-wife is up first," Wyatt said. "She's been gracious enough to let me choose her song."

Linnea poked him in the ribs. "I know how much he loves *Same Spell Next Year* by the Magicians."

"It's a paranormal band," Alec said to me. "You won't have heard of them in the human world."

Hank handled the drinks and the karaoke setup with ease. Linnea took her place on the stage and blew everyone away with her rendition of the song. Although the tune was wholly unfamiliar to me, I could tell by the rapturous expressions that my cousin was knocking it out of the park.

Wyatt whistled, seemingly starstruck by his ex-wife's

performance. "Goddess of the Moon, she's amazing, ain't she?"

"She really is," I replied. "Does she do karaoke often?"

"Used to," he said. "We'd go together on Friday nights years ago. Linnea looked like an angel up there, with that serene expression and such a heavenly voice."

"Why did she stop?" I asked.

His expression soured. "Why else? Because of me, of course. I disappeared with the barmaids one too many times. Linnea was too horrified to show her face. I humiliated her with my selfishness."

Opposite Wyatt was very insightful.

"Do you regret it?" I asked.

"Every day," he replied, without hesitation. "If I had the power to go back in time…" He shook his head ruefully. "Linnea's too good for me, though. Always was. I think that's why I acted out. Deep down, I wanted her to chuck me because I knew I didn't deserve her."

Typical Wyatt would squelch his sense of inadequacy and replace it with bravado. Opposite spell Wyatt was willing to admit his failures and acknowledge the reasons behind them.

"You're very in touch with your emotions these days, brother," Sheriff Nash said. "What's gotten into you?"

"Regret," Wyatt said. "Regret has settled into my cheating heart."

Linnea stepped off the stage to a noisy round of applause, oblivious to Wyatt's admission. He engulfed her in a hug and she beamed with pride. I was definitely holding off on reversing the spell for now. Linnea deserved this special treatment by her ex-husband.

"I've really missed that," she said. "I need to sing more often." She kissed Wyatt's cheek. "Thank you for thinking of this. It was a lovely idea."

"You singing tonight, Hale?" Sheriff Nash asked. The

implication was clear: Alec was not the type of vampire to sing karaoke.

"As a matter fact, I already have my song selected." Alec looked at Hank. "You have *Born to Run*, do you not?"

My heart soared. "You're going to sing Bruce Springsteen?"

A smile tugged at his lips. "I thought you might appreciate the choice."

The sheriff's jaw set. "How about *Born in the USA*? Do you have that one?"

Hank brightened. "We can do any song you like. The karaoke offerings are infinite."

Wyatt swallowed his ale and wiped his mouth with his sleeve. "A Springsteen showdown. This ought to be good."

I couldn't decide whether I was entertained or embarrassed by the prospect. I knew the vampire and the werewolf had a rocky history, so I wasn't sure how much of their competition tonight was related to me.

Alec rose from the stool with his usual grace. "I shall go first. Someone needs to set the bar high."

Sheriff Nash barked a short laugh. "We'll have to wait about three more minutes for that."

I tightened my grip on the glass of ale. This was not the evening I expected it to be.

Alec stepped onto the stage like he was a born performer. It was a whole new side to him. His velvety voice transformed into a raspy sound that belonged to an aging rock star, rather than an ageless vampire. Suddenly, the crowd in front of the stage multiplied. All conversation ceased as everyone stopped to listen. I cast a sidelong glance at Sheriff Nash. The werewolf stood rooted in silence, sucking down his ale. I had no doubt he was regretting his threats of one-upmanship.

I moved to stand beside him. "You don't have to sing Springsteen. You could choose someone else."

The sheriff looked at me like I was nuts. "You think this guy can out-Springsteen me? I'm the jeans and boots guy. He looks like he's wearing a Halloween costume."

I suppressed a laugh. The vampire was well known for his custom suits and expensive taste.

I watched Alec perform the rest of the song and couldn't help but be impressed by his vocals and stage presence. His ninja moves truly came into their own. His body was impressive enough in a tailored suit. In jeans and a T-shirt, it was jaw-droppingly amazing.

"So is this a date?" the sheriff asked. I'd wondered how long it would take for him to ask that question.

"Honestly, I don't know what it is," I said. I couldn't tell the sheriff about the spell, even though I knew it would make him feel better.

"Just out of curiosity, how many of us are there?" the sheriff asked.

I shot him a quizzical look. "How many of what?"

"Guys where you don't really know how to define your relationship."

I bristled. "I know how to define all of my relationships," I said. "Alec Hale is my boss and a friend. You're the sheriff, whom I sometimes work alongside for purposes of a story. See? No ambiguity there."

"Speaking of work, I wanted to mention a report that came across my desk."

"Something to do with the Maitland boy?" I asked.

"Not sure. A fairy called Kelsey complained about teenagers messing with her stable of unicorns the same night as the murder. Deputy Bolan handled the incident report."

"Unicorns?" I echoed.

"Yeah, you know unicorns. Like horses but with a single horn…"

I punched him in the gut. "I know what a unicorn is, smart mouth."

He laughed as he clutched his stomach. "How should I know? You're from New Jersey." He winced. "As you've just proven with your unprovoked violence."

"Ha! You call that violence? You've never been outside a Best Buy on Black Friday."

The song ended and everyone cheered wildly. Sheriff Nash cracked his knuckles. "Time for the real show."

It didn't take long for me to realize the sheriff lacked Alec and Linnea's singing talent. To his credit, Alec remained silent, his expression placid. It didn't matter, though. I could tell by the pained look on the sheriff's face that he *knew* he was terrible.

I leaned over to Linnea and whispered, "Is there a spell we can do to make him better?" It was awkward enough that I was out with Alec. I didn't want the sheriff to be humiliated under the spotlight as well.

Linnea made a twirling motion with her finger and said a Latin phrase under her breath. The only word I understood was 'Springsteen.' Suddenly, the sheriff's posture changed and his vocals improved. If I closed my eyes, it sounded like Bruce Springsteen himself was performing for the crowd in Strange Brew. Amazing.

"Quite impressive," Alec said. "Almost as though he's been practicing."

"I doubt it," I said. "I think he's a natural, like you."

Alec grinned. "Thank you, Ember. Your compliments mean more than you realize."

Heat pooled in my stomach. The way Alec looked at me was distracting enough to make me forget the perfect performance happening in front of us.

"Ember," Alec said slowly, dragging out each letter. His eyes bored into mine. "How would you like to come back to my place for a drink? I make an excellent poisoned apple martini." He winked. "No actual poison required."

"You're inviting me back to your place?" I queried. I knew it was the spell. The real Alec would never invite me into his private space. He was too protective of himself.

He snaked an arm around my waist. "I understand if you'd rather not."

Although I should have, I didn't hesitate. I hopped off the stool. "I'd rather."

His brow lifted. "You're certain?"

I grabbed his hand. "Let's go before one of us changes our mind."

In the end, I was the one who changed my mind. It felt wrong to take advantage of Alec while he was under a spell. Even though I knew the feelings he expressed were genuine, he'd never have chosen this course of action without a magical nudge. He wanted to keep me at arm's length, not *in* his arms and I had to respect that.

We'd only made it as far as the entryway of his house before the kissing began. He lifted me like I was weightless and pressed me against the wall, gently exploring the curve of my neck with his fangs. When I felt a slight prick, I cried out, but it was in pleasure rather than pain. I'd been wanting to have this experience with him since the moment I met him. With my legs wrapped around his waist and my lips nibbling all available real estate, I was in heaven. It was only when he began to carry me toward what I assumed was the bedroom that my mind cleared. He'd never forgive himself if he went through with this. Once I reversed the spell, he'd be mortified.

It took all my strength to stop kissing him. It was, in all honesty, one of the hardest things I ever had to do.

"I need to go, Alec," I said, sliding down the length of his body until my feet hit the floor.

His hands were still tangled in my hair and our lips were equally swollen. Okay, mine were a little more swollen thanks to his fangs getting in the way. He couldn't keep them retracted no matter how hard he tried.

"The bathroom is this way," he said in a raspy voice.

"No, I don't need to pee," I said, although I wasn't surprised by his assumption. Everyone knew my bladder was the size of a pumpkin seed. "I need to go home."

He released his hold on me. "Home? Are you certain?"

I gazed into his eyes and pondered the question. As much as I wanted to stay, I was certain I had to leave.

"I'm sorry, Alec. It's for the best." My chest tightened. What was I doing?

He traced my jaw with his thumb. "Did I do something to upset you?"

"Of course not," I replied. "I worry you might regret this later, and I don't want that."

He pressed his forehead against mine. "There is something very special between us, Ember. We've been foolish to suppress our feelings."

Ugh. Yes, that was how *I* felt, but I knew perfectly well that wasn't how 'normal' Alec viewed the situation.

"Like I said, it's for the best." I gave him a quick kiss on the lips and darted out the door before I had a change of heart. Ever the gentleman, Alec didn't try to stop me.

Tears streaked my cheeks as I signaled for his driver to take me home. As we passed through town, I stared out the window at the night sky, silently taking myself to task for this mess. If I hadn't wanted to play a joke on Hazel, none of this would have happened. I'd potentially destroyed my relationships with both Alec and the sheriff and for what? A hot make-out session? Was I a teenager all over again where hormones ruled the day? I touched the spot on my neck where his fangs had pierced me and sighed. Despite the pang of regret I felt over the incident, there was something to be said for heightened emotions. They reminded me of what I was capable of feeling—the highs and the lows. They reminded me that, although Karl was dead, I was still very much alive.

CHAPTER 16

I LINKED arms with Aster and entered the impressive marble building that served as the Silver Moon coven headquarters. We passed through the six enormous columns at the front and I tilted my head up to admire the barefoot witch statue on the rooftop. I smiled, thinking of Sheriff Nash and his fear of heights.

"Five minutes to spare," Aster said. "Mother will be pleased." Aunt Hyacinth did not tolerate tardiness or social missteps of any kind. As the *de facto* head of the coven, she preferred to set the standard for the rest of the members.

"Good evening, Dillon," I said. Dillon Stanton-Summer was Wren's fraternal twin and the Watchman, the head of security for the coven.

"Good evening, witches," Dillon said. "Any items to declare?"

"Just our handbags," I said. "If you feel like thumbing through tampons and a packet of tissues, be my guest."

He grinned. "You're not going to put me off with talk of lady products. I'm a pro." He wiggled his fingers. "Let's see."

We handed him our bags and he gave them a quick sweep before returning them.

"No Sterling tonight?" he asked.

"Not tonight," Aster said. "He's working late and then promised to be home to tuck the boys into bed."

"Sterling is the hardest working wizard in Starry Hollow," Dillon said. "It's a shame he doesn't put the same effort into his family."

Ooh, snap.

Aster maintained her regal air. "Come along, Ember. Time to mix with the rest of the coven."

Across the room, I glimpsed Argyle Pennywhistle, the Purse Warden. He was an elderly wizard with thinning gray hair and a pinched expression.

"If it isn't the beautiful descendants of the One True Witch," a voice sang. Camille Poppywick appeared in my line of vision. The musical director, or the Bard as she was known in the coven, attempted to wrap me in a bear hug. Thankfully, I managed to extricate myself without losing consciousness.

"Nice to see you again, Camille," I said.

She studied me. "Please tell me you've reconsidered the opportunity to participate in the musical this year."

"Can't say that I have," I said. "I'm surprised Linnea doesn't want to sign up, though. Her voice is incredible."

Aster gently kicked the back of my heel. Oops.

"Linnea?" Camille frowned. "Any time I've heard her sing, she sounds completely tone deaf."

No doubt because she was trying to hide her talent from Camille.

"You know, I don't have much of an ear," I said. "If I think someone sounds great, they probably sound like a dying cat." I spotted Wren as he threaded his way through the crowd.

Just the wizard I needed to see. "Excuse me. I need to grab Wren before the meeting starts. A question about our last lesson."

He raised a thick eyebrow when he saw me coming. "You've got that determined look. Should I be concerned?"

I tried to relax my facial features. "Sorry. What my brain is thinking usually gets translated by my face. They're in cahoots."

His mouth twitched. "Yes, I'm familiar with your fascinating variety of facial expressions. What's up?"

I glanced around furtively before responding. "Remember the spell you taught me? The special one to calm a certain crazed clown?"

His brow furrowed. "Did it misfire?"

"I haven't used it on her yet," I whispered. "But I may have accidentally used it on someone else. How long before it wears off?"

Wren sucked in a breath. "It doesn't wear off, Ember. You need to reverse it."

Right. "Okay, so how do I do that?"

Wren fixated on me. "Do I need to get involved?"

"No, absolutely not," I reassured him. "I can handle it. I just need to know what to do."

"You focus your will and make sure it's clear that you're reversing the opposite spell. Then you point your wand and say 'novis.'"

"*Novis?*" I repeated.

"That's right." He hesitated. "Do I want to know who the unfortunate victim is?"

"Probably best if I'm the only one with that information," I said. "Don't worry, Wren. I'll fix it. Promise."

He pointed a finger at me. "You'd better, Ember. I don't want this blowing back on me. I did you a favor."

"I know and I appreciate it." And if I wanted him to keep doing me favors, I had to take care of this mess without any fallout. "I've got it under control, Master."

He chuckled. "Oh, I do like it when you call me that."

Ringing bells signaled the start of the meeting. I entered the cavernous hall and marveled once again at the hundreds of candles that lined the room. Three was a sacred number to the coven. There were three candlelit chandeliers dangling from the ceiling. Three enormous wooden tables in the middle of the hall. Three women that represented the phases of life — the Maiden, the Mother, and the Crone.

I sat beside Aster at the front of the room, along with Linnea, Aunt Hyacinth, and Florian. I surveyed the area for familiar faces. Every month, I recognized more and more. I smiled when I noticed Delphine, the librarian, seated at the far end of the table wearing a bright shade of pink gloss.

"Delphine looks pretty tonight," I said, mainly for Florian's benefit.

His gaze meandered around the room. "Who's Delphine?"

I grimaced. Naturally, Florian didn't remember the librarian. Next time I'd suggest that she douse herself in glitter.

A softer bell rang to introduce the High Priestess, Iris Sandstone. She swept into the hall in her silver cloak, her silver moon crown glistening on her head. She took her place at the head table and gave thanks to the Goddess of the Moon. Flames flickered and I felt a tiny thrill as the meeting began.

"The monthly Silver Moon coven meeting is now called to order."

I noticed Gardenia, the Scribe, busily typing notes on her iPhone. The Purse Warden gave the financial report and, finally, the floor was open to new business. Aunt Hyacinth stood and everyone gave her their full attention. I'd never seen someone with such a commanding presence.

"My lovely coven," she began. "I come this evening bearing joyous news. My niece, Ember Rose, has been united with her familiar."

The coven broke into a round of applause. I was surprised that my aunt chose to acknowledge the existence of Raoul, since she seemed so aghast that he wasn't a cat.

"She is making tremendous strides in her training," my aunt continued, and I caught the amused look on Hazel's face. I stuck out my tongue and Hazel promptly tried to suppress her fit of giggles.

"Now that she's made the acquaintance of her familiar, we can begin her training in the Familiar Arts." She stretched out her arm toward a man at the middle table. "As the Master-in-Familiar Arts, Ian will oversee her lessons in this area. We expect a favorable progress report at the next coven meeting."

I jerked my head toward my aunt. Wait. Another training session? My schedule was already busting at the seams. When was I going to fit in Ian and what on earth did a Master-in-Familiar Arts do?

"It will be my pleasure," Ian piped up. He sounded congested and I winced at the thought of his post-nasal drip in my cottage.

"Thank you, Hyacinth," Iris said. "Are we to hear from anyone else this evening?"

Lee, the Master-of-Ritual Toolcraft, scraped back his chair and stood. "Has there been an update on the murder investigation involving the young elf? I was going to take my kids to see the sand sculptures, but I thought it best to wait until we knew more about his death."

Heads turned to each other. I felt Linnea's foot press the

top of mine under the table and I shot her a sharp look. Did she want me to speak on behalf of the sheriff?

"Speak for *Vox Populi*," Linnea whispered, as though reading my thoughts.

I stood awkwardly. "There's a full investigation happening as we speak." In my effort to be heard, I ended up sounding like I was screeching my response. Beside me, Aster winced. Florian wore his usual amused expression.

"Are there any leads?" he asked.

"I can't comment on a pending investigation," I said. "I can tell you in my pursuit of the story for *Vox Populi*, that the sheriff has the situation well in hand."

"Is that because he has you well in hand?" someone interjected.

There was a smattering of laughter.

"No one has me well in hand," I snapped.

"Is it true that you and the sheriff are dating?" another voice asked. "I heard you were spotted on a broomstick together."

My hands flew to my hips. "Keep your pointy hats on. It was for purposes of the investigation, not a declaration of undying love."

My aunt raised a finger to her lips and silenced the room. "My niece's romantic entanglements are her business. She is covering the murder for the family paper, and that puts her in the path of the sheriff quite often. That does not mean they're in a relationship. It only means they have reasons to interact with each other on a regular basis." She placed an earnest hand on her chest. "Let's be honest. Everyone here knows I prefer my niece to find a partner within the coven."

Oh no, she didn't. I should have known she would pull a stunt like this. She was making a power play right here in front of the whole coven. Then again, I fired the warning shot when I told her I'd date whomever I pleased and that I didn't need her approval. This was clearly her way of putting me in my place.

I fumed for the remainder of the meeting. Waves of anger crested and flattened inside me. How dare she? I wasn't one of her children. I'd been on my own for my entire adult life, and I had no intention of living under anyone's thumb, no matter how powerful that thumb was.

"You look ready to spit fire," Aster said at the end of the meeting. Aunt Hyacinth had vacated her seat to network with Iris. My aunt was no fool. She knew I'd want to confront her.

"Your mother seems to think she can bend me to her will," I said. "I'm telling you right now that it's not happening."

"Oh, please tell her off now," Florian begged. "I really want to see this unfold."

"I don't need to tell her off," I said. Actions spoke louder than words. I'd simply continue to date outside the coven. That would set her straight. Eventually.

"Ember, I look forward to our training sessions." Ian stood in front of me with a bright red nose. Great, now he'd forever be called Rudolph in my twisted mind.

"I'll have to see when I can squeeze you into the schedule," I said. "I'm pretty booked right now."

Ian wagged his finger at me. "Don't put off until tomorrow what you can do today, Ember. You owe it to your familiar to learn this part of the craft."

"I can already talk to him more than I care to," I said. "What else will you teach me?"

Ian's eyes brightened. "We'll go through elementals, totems, shapeshifting..."

"What's a totem?" I asked. "Like those carved faces outside caves in Indiana Jones movies?"

Ian blinked. "I don't know what an Indiana Jones movie is, but totems can be guardian spirits. Sometimes objects are imbued with these spirits, which may be what you're referencing with these carved faces."

"There are spirits in the wooden statues?" I asked, slightly confused.

"Perhaps. You can call upon spirits to manifest in these objects," Ian said. "That's one of the lessons."

I didn't love the idea of calling upon spirits to manifest in any way, shape, or form. "How do you do it?" I asked. I didn't want to accidentally summon one into the cottage. What if it manifested in my crockpot by mistake? My cooking already tended toward disaster.

"Let's save it for the lesson, shall we?" Ian suggested. He pulled a plaid handkerchief from his pocket and dabbed at his nostrils one at a time. Ugh.

"Go on, Ian," Florian urged. "Give her a preview. She's clearly not interested. It's your job to make it worth her while." He pointed to the figurine of the Goddess of the Moon on the main table. "Use that as a totem."

Ian stuffed his handkerchief back into his pocket and retrieved his wand. "You take aim, of course."

Florian blew out a breath. "Great gods of thunder, man. She's not a moron."

Ian's cheeks flamed. "I have no idea how far along she's progressed. Hazel says…" He stopped talking.

"Yes, yes," I said. "I'm the laziest witch on the planet and not fit to carry the Rose name."

"Ah, so you're in agreement," Ian said, and Florian chuckled.

"Please continue, Ian," I said.

Ian pointed his wand at the goddess figurine and said, "*Anima*."

My eyebrows shot up when the figurine waved to us. "It's alive?" I asked, aghast.

"Not in any real sense," Ian said. "It's a temporary spiritual occupation." He gestured to the figurine. "Come forward, please."

The pint-sized goddess jumped off the table's edge and came rushing over to us, eager to serve.

"See? Fun, but pointless," Florian said.

Ian tried to hide his humiliation.

"I think it's pretty cool," I said.

Ian glanced up hopefully. "Really?"

"Absolutely." I kneeled down and offered the tiny goddess a fist bump. "Marley will think I'm the greatest mom ever if I can animate her toys with spirits. No more imaginary friends."

Ian blew his nose. "I'm not sure that's really the intent…"

Florian clapped the wizard on the back. "Now it's time for your lesson, Ian. When a woman tells you something's cool, just roll with it."

Ian's chin jerked up and down. "Duly noted. I'll endeavor to make it worth your time, Ember. And be sure to include your familiar. What's the name again?"

"Raoul," I said. "He's a raccoon."

Ian seemed unperturbed. "Yes, yes. Splendid. I've never worked with a raccoon before. New opportunities abound for all of us."

Well, at least one of us was excited.

"I can't work you in this week, Ian," I said truthfully. With the investigation into Grover's death in full swing, I wasn't willing to add another coven item to my burgeoning list. "But soon. I promise."

Ian waved his wand at the figurine and she returned to her normal state. I plucked her from the floor and placed her back on the table.

"I guess you're never lonely, Ian," I joked.

"It's impossible to be lonely when one is connected to the universe," Ian said.

Holy smokes. He was as earnest as they came.

Ian tucked away his wand. "We all have lessons to teach in this world. Perhaps I'll learn from you as well."

I sighed. "I don't know, Ian. The things I can teach you, you probably don't want to learn."

CHAPTER 17

I STOOD at the edge of the field, speechless. Marley elbowed me multiple times before I had the wherewithal to look at her.

"Unicorns," she said in a hushed, reverent tone.

"I can see that." In fact, I could see about a dozen of them, prancing and galloping around the open space like garden-variety horses.

"I only see silver horns and white horns," Marley said. "For some reason, I thought there'd be gold ones."

"You're staring at a dozen of every little girl's dream animal and you're complaining about the color of their horns?" I asked, with a shake of my head. "Where did I go wrong?"

"Golden horns are only found on sacred unicorns," a voice said. "They are a rare and special breed."

I forced my attention away from the dream animals and focused on the fairy fluttering in front of me. Her cropped hair was lime green hair and her pale skin was powdered with glitter.

"These are your unicorns?" I asked.

"Sure are. I'm the Kelsey in Kelsey's Stables," the fairy said. "Have you come to ride?"

I stared at the unicorns in awe. We could ride them? "Um, not exactly."

"But we will after we've asked our questions," Marley blurted. "Right, Mom?"

"I don't see how we could let the opportunity pass us by," I said. Aside from the fact that Marley would never forgive me, I wanted to ride one.

Kelsey's teeth gleamed in the sunlight. "What's your question, honey?"

"I understand you filed a report with the sheriff's office recently," I said.

She scowled. "Sure did. I caught some teenagers trying to slice off one of my unicorn's horns. Can you imagine? They were as high as flying broomsticks."

"But they ran off before you could identify them?" I queried.

She nodded, clearly annoyed. "I tried to do a spell to freeze them, but I wasn't fast enough." Slowly, she rotated her wrist. "Arthritis."

"Why would they want to hurt the unicorn?" Marley asked, distressed by the thought.

"I don't know for sure that they intended to hurt him," Kelsey said. "I assume it was about money. Unicorn horns are valuable, although not as valuable as sacred unicorn horns. Those have magical healing properties."

Healing properties? The gears of mind began clicking away. "Like vampire blood?"

Kelsey's laugh sounded like a tinkling bell. "Far more potent. That's one of the main reasons the sacred unicorn is so prized."

"The sheriff's report said there were three of them," I said. "Any identifying information?"

"No, but one of them was incredibly fast," Kelsey said. "No wings either, which made the speed more impressive."

"Maybe a vampire?" Marley asked. "They're supposed to have super speed, right?"

Kelsey shook her head. "I wish I knew. It was dark and they took me by surprise. I'm not as young as I used to be."

"How do you know they were high?" I asked.

"Their speech was slurred and they were in a panic before they even realized I was there," Kelsey explained. "Everything seemed heightened."

"But you haven't had any incidents since then?" I asked.

"No," Kelsey said. "But I've placed a ward around the field. It activates at night. I never felt the need to do that before, so it's disappointing." She gave a sad smile. "But that's the world we live in now, I guess."

I observed two unicorns sparring with their horns. "Are they fighting?"

Kelsey followed my gaze. "No, they're playing. They're truly wonderful creatures. I don't know what I would've done if one of them had been harmed on my watch. They're my responsibility."

"And they don't mind being ridden?" Marley asked.

"Not at all," Kelsey said. "They're tame." She whistled and one of the unicorns trotted over. "This is Magnus. How would you feel about riding him?"

Marley's blue eyes popped at the sight of the impressive unicorn. "Can we?"

"Would you like to ride together or separately?" Kelsey asked. "Either is fine."

I looked at Marley, uncertain what her response would be.

"I'd like to ride him on my own, if that's okay," Marley said, with a hesitant glance in my direction.

Inwardly, I was ecstatic. If Marley wanted to do this on

her own, I was all for it. "Sure," I said nonchalantly. "Whatever you want."

Kelsey used her fairy wand to lift Marley onto the unicorn's broad back.

"No saddle?" I queried.

"No, unicorns are ridiculously comfortable," Kelsey said. "Like sitting on a velvet cushion."

Marley shifted her bottom from side to side. "It's true, Mom."

"Do you have any pegasi?" I asked. The idea of a flying horse was incredibly appealing.

"None in my stables," Kelsey said. "Unicorns only. My cousin Rinaldo keeps pegasi if you're interested."

"Not today," I said. "I'll join Marley in the field."

Kelsey whistled again and another unicorn galloped to her side. "This is Princess. She's a real beauty."

From her muscled legs to her sleek mane, Princess was exquisite. Kelsey waved her wand and I floated onto the unicorn's back.

"Nice to meet you, Princess," I said, and she whinnied gently in response.

Kelsey squinted. "Wow. She doesn't normally talk back like that. She must really like you."

I thought of my family's horses—Bell, Book, and Candle—and Florian's surprise when Candle seemed to understand everything I said.

"I seem to have an affinity for animals," I said.

"Her familiar is a raccoon," Marley said proudly.

Kelsey inclined her head. "A raccoon. How…interesting." I could tell she was mildly appalled. "Enjoy the ride, girls!"

Marley and I rode around the field, enjoying every moment of this magical experience. At one point, colorful butterflies surrounded us, all clamoring to get close to our unicorns. It seemed we weren't the only ones obsessed with these fantastic beasts. Marley was in her element and I felt a surge of pride as I watched her ride by herself.

"This is amazing," she called to me.

It really was. The unicorns had to be the most majestic creatures I'd ever seen. I gazed at the silver horn on my unicorn's head, longing to touch it, but I wasn't sure what the etiquette was. Maybe it was like touching a pregnant woman's belly without permission. A definite no-no.

"Um, Princess, would you mind if I touched your horn?" I felt ridiculous asking, but I didn't know what else to do. Princess slowed to a canter and tilted back her head, seeming to understand my request. I reached up and ran my fingers down the shiny horn.

Marley drew Magnus alongside us. "Can we do this again sometime?"

Kelsey fluttered over to us. "Your daughter seems like a natural. If you're interested, I offer lessons. Lots of young girls learn unicorn riding. I've trained quite a few that went on to compete in national events and received college scholarships."

That sounded great—but also expensive. "Thanks, we'll have to think about it," I said.

"It costs a lot, huh?" Marley said, not one to beat around the bush.

Kelsey smiled. "I'm sure we can work something out. My primary concern is that I have a rider worthy of the unicorn, and I think you've ticked that box."

"I bet Aunt Hyacinth would pay for it," Marley said.

"Marley!" I said quickly. I didn't want her to grow up expecting Aunt Hyacinth to support us. It was one thing to give us a leg up after leaving New Jersey so unexpectedly. At some point, though, we had to be able to stand on our own two feet.

"Hyacinth Rose-Muldoon?" Kelsey queried. "She's your aunt?"

"I'm her brother's daughter," I said.

Kelsey stared at me in wonder. "Of course. How did I miss it?"

"Well, it's easy since I don't look like a magical supermodel," I replied.

Kelsey clasped her hands in front of her. "No, you look exactly as you should. You look like your mother."

My heart lifted. "You knew my mother?"

Kelsey nodded happily. "Oh, honey. I did, indeed. She used to ride here, in fact."

"How is that possible?" I asked. "You don't look much older than me."

"Fairy blood," she replied. "It may not have healing properties like vampire blood, but it keeps us looking youthful."

I shook my head in amazement. "You're not kidding."

Kelsey shifted her attention to Marley. "I'll tell you what, Marley. Why don't you take a few lessons and see how you enjoy it? If you love it, we'll make arrangements that suit you. If not, you got to try something new. Does that sound like a good plan?"

Marley looked to me for approval.

"Are you sure, Kelsey?" I asked. "We don't want to take advantage…"

"Your mother was an excellent rider," Kelsey said. "If Marley has even a fraction of her talent, and I suspect she may, I'll be lucky to have her here. It makes good business sense for the stables."

If nothing else, it would get Marley out of the sedentary position. As much as I loved her reading obsession, I knew it was important for her to be active.

"You have a deal," I said, and Marley squealed with delight.

"Are you sure Sierra comes here every Thursday night?" Florian asked.

My cousin and I sat at the bar of the Whitethorn, an old pub between Fairy Cove and the Lighthouse. It was so close to the sea, you could taste the salt in the air every time you drew breath. Residents claimed you could feel ancient magic clinging to the air there, like heavy fog.

"According to Rick, yes," I whispered.

"Your new minotaur friend?" he asked.

"You should meet him," I said quietly. "He's very nice. I actually think he might hit it off with Linnea."

Florian choked back laughter. "I'd give anything to see Mother's reaction to Linnea dating a minotaur, as though a werewolf weren't bad enough."

"Rick is no ordinary minotaur," I assured him in a hushed tone.

"Why do you keep whispering?" Florian asked. "No one else is here."

I gestured helplessly to Captain Yellowjacket behind the bar. "His parrot has a big mouth."

"Just the way I like my women," Bittersteel squawked from his perch. "Big in every way."

I covered my face with my hand. "Is there no sexual harassment policy in this place?"

Captain Yellowjacket stepped in front of his feathered companion. "He doesn't get out much, Ember."

"Maybe you should remedy that," I said. "Like right now."

On cue, the door blew open and Sierra stepped inside, along with two friends. One was a shifter of some kind and the other was the genie I recognized from Haverford House. The one with the disappointing outcome for his love life, at least according to the runes. Our eyes met briefly and a hint of recognition flashed in his eyes. He drifted over to hover next to my stool.

"Evenin', Captain," he said. "I'd like a round of crackle-berry ales for my friends, including these two beauties right here." He smacked the counter in front of me and I jumped.

"That's nice of you," I said.

"Any friend of Artemis Haverford's is a friend of mine," he said. "I've been going to see her for years."

"My name's Ember and this is my cousin, Florian."

"I recognize a Rose-Muldoon when I see one," he said, his attention fixed on my godlike cousin. "I'm Geoff and that's Sierra and Fargo."

I waved to Sierra, who had settled into a booth with Fargo. "Yes, she and I met recently. She owns the ceramics place."

"That's right," Geoff said. "Does a booming business, too. Her garden gnomes are known all over the world. Some gardener even features them in her YouTube videos."

"Really?" I didn't realize it was a worldwide business. They didn't seem particularly special. They looked like garden gnomes I'd seen in the human world.

"Oh, yes," Geoff said, stopping to swill his ale. "She even gets custom orders from higher-ups in the paranormal world."

I shot a quizzical look at Florian. "There are higher-ups?"

My cousin took a nonchalant sip of ale. "There are always higher-ups."

"What makes them so popular?" I asked. I was always intrigued by trends. I knew all about Cabbage Patch dolls in the Eighties from my dad. Their insane popularity remained a mystery me.

"*Paranormal Monthly* featured the gardens of Queen Alinor and there were two of Sierra's garden gnomes on display. Sales skyrocketed after that. The fairy queen is beloved in the paranormal world."

Florian nodded. "The copycat phenomenon is very real. I remember a phase where residents here were dying their hair white-blond to look like one of us."

Geoff chuckled. "I remember that. My ex-girlfriend was one of them. She quickly got fed up with the roots growing in and switched back when one of the hair tonics burned her scalp."

Florian patted his own head. "It's good to be natural."

"Why don't you join us?" Geoff asked. "It seems a shame not to, as we're the only ones here tonight."

"Sounds good to me," I said. Without an attractive female to hit on, I was half expecting Florian to ditch me. To his credit, he stuck with the plan. He was eager to get to the bottom of Grover's murder, too. Anything to shift the spotlight back to the sand sculpture competition.

We settled into the large booth with Sierra and Fargo. They seemed to be deep in conversation about some town called Spellbound and why the paranormals were trapped there. Whatever the reason was, they didn't seem to agree on it.

Geoff cleared his throat. "Fargo, Sierra, meet my new friends, Ember Rose and her cousin..."

"Florian Rose-Muldoon," Sierra interjected. She stuck out her hand. "Good to meet you. I've always wanted to see these cheekbones up close and, oh my, they are as divine as I imagined."

"I must've inherited my mother's cheekbones," I said, absently touching my face.

"You're a Rose," Sierra said, taking a renewed interest in me. "With your coloring, I didn't realize you were one of *the* Roses."

"I only discovered it myself recently," I admitted. "I grew up in the human world." I generally found that if I offered a bit of personal information about me, I got personal details in return. Although Sierra certainly seemed to have no shortage of things to say, I was on the hunt for specific intel.

"Where in the human world?" Sierra asked.

"New Jersey," I replied.

"Interesting. I have a lot of contacts there." Sierra poured the ale down her throat like she'd just come from a week in the Sahara.

"Because of the ceramics business?" I queried.

"That's right. My distribution is in the human world and the paranormal one," Sierra said. "I don't like to be constrained by societal norms."

Florian laughed. "Then I highly advise you to steer clear of my mother because I'm fairly certain she invented societal norms."

"I met your mother at a coven fundraiser once," Sierra said. "I spoke to her about popular garden plants. In my line of work, you learn all about the plants, as well the planters."

I bet.

"You'd be amazed by the custom requests I've gotten," she continued. "Usually they want the gnomes to look like them. They send me pictures of their spouses, or kids, or whatever."

I snickered at the idea of having a garden gnome made in Aunt Hyacinth's image. A gnome wearing a kaftan with cat faces on it. Glorious!

"What's so funny?" Florian asked.

"I have an idea for your mother's birthday," I said. "You'll have to tell me when it is."

"Mother doesn't celebrate birthdays," he said. "She finds it lowbrow."

Of course she did.

Sierra snapped her fingers impatiently. "Yellowjacket, where's the next round? You're slacking off, vam-pirate, and you know I can't tolerate incompetence."

I recoiled slightly. Captain Yellowjacket was descended from Blackfang, the most fearsome vampire pirate in history. Even I didn't have the stones to snap my fingers at him.

Captain Yellowjacket seemed unperturbed by Sierra's behavior, although I did catch his parrot making gagging gestures behind the bar. Not a fan of the valkyrie's, presumably.

Once she was good and tipsy, I attempted to extract the information I wanted.

"I thought of you last night when my daughter wanted to renegotiate the terms of her bedtime," I lied. "She hasn't even hit eleven yet and I'm ready to throttle her half the time. Yet you work with teenagers every day and live to tell the tale."

"That's because I know how to keep them in line," she said with a loud hiccup.

"Of course you do," Fargo said. "You're Sierra, the valkyrie."

"Stop kissing my ass, Fargo," she snapped. "It's annoying. Anyway, I've got teenagers coming and going at all hours, even when I'm not there, and they're never a lick of trouble."

"That's probably because they're afraid of you," Geoff said. "You're not exactly the sweet and cuddly type."

"You didn't object to my type the other night," Sierra shot back.

I cringed as Geoff's face turned beet red. "You must have to monitor them, though," I said, steering the conversation back to teenagers.

"Yes," Florian said quickly. He seemed to catch on to where I was heading. "I'd bet another round of ale they steal from you and you don't even notice. They probably go in at night when no one's there."

Sierra slammed a fist onto the table. "Minotaur shit! They wouldn't dare steal from me."

I gave a nonchalant shrug. "I don't know. Kids tend to think they're invincible."

"There are only three teenagers with the codes to deactivate my wards," Sierra said, holding up three fingers. "And I have an iron grip on all three."

And I bet I knew exactly which three teens she meant. "Why give the codes to any of them? That's more trust than I would have."

"Some of them need to come and go at odd hours," Sierra said. "I'm not hauling my ass over there on Friday at midnight to check on..." She waved a dismissive hand. "Inventory."

"You're usually too drunk by midnight, anyway," Fargo said, with the laugh of a deranged hyena. Hmm. Come to think of it, maybe he was a werehyena.

Sierra jabbed him in the chest with her elbow. "I'm not a drunk. You're the one who fell off the broomstick at that wizard's birthday party."

Fargo smiled at the memory. "Plunged straight into the ocean. The water felt good."

Geoff seemed to be the only one keeping his wits about him. "You're lucky you didn't drown."

"We like living on the edge, Geoff," Sierra said. "You should try it sometime."

"I, for one, don't like living anywhere near the edge," I said. "In fact, if I don't stop drinking now, I'm going to have the worst hangover. Florian, would you mind if we headed home?"

He shot to his feet like he'd been waiting to leave for hours. "Your wish is my command."

"Hey, that's my line," Geoff objected with a wry smile. He seemed like a decent genie. I hoped he wasn't tangled up in whatever Sierra had going on. If so, there wasn't much I could do to help him.

"It was nice chatting with you all," I said.

"Be sure to come by and choose a gnome," Sierra said to Florian. "I'd love to be able to tell prospective buyers that Florian Rose-Muldoon keeps one in his famous bachelor pad. Maybe I could even come and see it in person. Snap a few naked pictures. You could always hold the gnome in front of the family jewels, if you're feeling modest."

Florian flashed a good-natured smile. "I'll have to get back to you on that." He steered me toward the door, the smile still plastered across his gorgeous face. "You got what you came for?"

"Does a cauldron bubble?"

"Depends," Florian said. "If you've added an alkaline…"

I rolled my eyes. "Yes. The answer is yes." And Friday at midnight, I'd finally get to see what Sierra's teenaged employees were really paid to do.

CHAPTER 18

A‍T FIVE MINUTES TO MIDNIGHT, I waited outside Sierra's Ceramics, huddled in darkness. I wasn't sure which teenager I'd be dealing with until I saw the flash of crystal sparkling in the moonlight.

Spencer.

I observed the satyr as he approached the door and used his fingertips to type a code on the magical keypad. It glowed blue and the door swung open. I hurried in behind him just before the door clicked shut. If I'd been Indiana Jones, I wouldn't have had time to grab my hat.

I crept down the corridor, careful not to make a sound. Spencer headed for the main room, his hooves echoing on the linoleum floor. When I entered the room after him, rows and rows of garden gnomes stared back at me.

Spencer began to remove the lids one by one. It wasn't hard to guess what he intended to put inside.

I stayed in the shadows. He seemed able to operate by moonlight alone so the lights remained off. He went to one of the kilns and reached inside. Of course! The kiln was only a facade. There was no fire inside.

He grabbed a nearby box and began withdrawing bags from the kiln and chucking them into the box. Surely, Sierra could implement a better system than this. A little magic would've taken care of Spencer's tasks in about five minutes, but to include a magic user on a regular basis only increased the risk of discovery. Sierra probably guarded her secret like a dragon guarded its treasure.

I inhaled deeply and stepped into his line of sight. "That's quite a system you've got there, Spencer. Too bad you don't have any witches or fairies on your team to help out. It would be so much easier."

The satyr froze. "How…how did you get in here?"

"I followed you in when you deactivated the ward," I replied. "I guess you're the lucky penny tonight."

He dropped the box onto the floor and shut the door of the kiln. "I like to come here at night. It's quiet."

Nice try. "I bet your house is quiet in the middle of the night, too. No need to traipse all the way here."

"I get paid double," he said.

Now that made more sense.

"Even after what happened to Grover you keep coming here?" I asked. "How can you look yourself in the eye?"

Spencer's cheek muscle began to pulse. "That had nothing to do with working the night shift."

"No?" I queried. "I thought maybe Grover messed up a delivery and Sierra's not the forgiving kind, is she?"

"You've got it all wrong," he blurted, and then promptly clamped his mouth shut. He didn't want to risk saying too much.

"Then explain it to me," I said. "I was your age once. I remember what it's like to…" I trailed off, the gears clicking away in my head. Spencer was telling the truth. This *wasn't* about making a mistake or shirking responsibility. This wasn't even about Sierra's illegal side business, although the two were connected. My mind flashed to images of Alec and me kissing and groping each other like two hormonal teenagers. My heart beat faster. I remembered the way I'd felt in his arms that night. The intense high.

"You okay, lady?" Spencer asked, taking a step backward.

"I remember what it's like to feel alive," I whispered. The realization crashed down on me and I couldn't believe the idea hadn't occurred to me until now. Jordy's dad. The immense pressure on Jordy to achieve.

"You should go," Spencer said uneasily.

I held up a finger. "Not until you tell me the truth." The dots were there, begging to be connected. This wasn't about the distribution of illegal substances. That business was only tangentially connected. Bruce was the key. The centaur was reliving the high of his youth, and dragging his daughter and her friends along for the dangerous ride. No doubt he missed the intensity of the games and had tried to replace it with something more illicit. Something that resulted in the death of an innocent elf.

"The truth is I don't know what happened to Grover," Spencer said.

I fixed Spencer with my hard stare. "His death was accidental, wasn't it?"

His fingers gripped the crystals on his necklace like he was searching for the answer there. "I just told you I don't know what happened. How would I know it was accidental?"

"Because you were there," I said, advancing toward him. "You, Jordy, and Aldo. And Bruce, of course. Can't forget the big guy. He's the reason why no one is talking, isn't it?" Sierra was intimidating, but it was the centaur that controlled their actions with a viselike grip. Their fear of Bruce outweighed their fear of the sheriff. I didn't blame them. Bruce Hoskins was an intimidating centaur. Put him on a team with a valkyrie like Sierra and those kids' lips were vacu-sealed.

"I don't know what you're talking about," Spencer said, his face drained of color. "I told the sheriff already. I saw Grover earlier that night, but he went home early. I have no idea how he died."

I ignored his lies. "You do know! You even went to the unicorn stables because you heard their horns have healing properties. You were desperate when the vampire blood didn't bring him back. Kelsey chased you off, but it wouldn't have mattered, you know. They weren't the right kind of unicorns. The horn wouldn't have made any difference."

I saw relief reflected in his soulful brown eyes. The idea that he could've saved his friend with the unicorn horn must have gnawed at him.

"Spencer," I said, injecting as much compassion into my tone as possible. "Grover was your friend. His family deserves to know the truth." I placed my hand on my wand as a preventative measure, in case those crystals were more than decorative. "Cindy deserves to know what happened to her brother. She blames herself. You don't want that on your conscience, do you?"

Spencer looked conflicted. When he finally spoke, his voice was barely audible. "No one checked the vampire blood supply before we started. Jordy had won a game earlier, so she and Bruce were distracted, talking about the championships."

"Tell me how it works," I prodded. "You came here to Sierra's because she has some kind of agreement with Bruce, right?" I wanted to know about the group's nocturnal activities—the real reason Grover was coming home in the middle of the night and slacking off at school.

He nodded, twisting his necklace. "Bruce figured out that she was using the gnomes to transport deadly plants and stuff, so he threatened to expose her unless she made a deal with him."

"So she agreed to let you keep a stash of your own," I said.

Spencer nodded. "Bruce got the idea about coding from his job."

"He works as a healer's assistant," I said, suddenly remembering.

"Yeah. Aldo's uncle got him a job because Aldo and Jordy were friends. Anyway, he treated some dryad last year after the dude almost died from nightshade and Bruce figured out how to bring him back with vamp blood without turning him into a vampire."

"And let me guess—the dryad he treated talked about some kind of heightened emotional experience."

Spencer's eyes grew round. "Totally. Like it was the most amazing experience of his life. Bruce wanted to try it, but he couldn't do it alone."

Inwardly, I cringed. "So he got Jordy to help?"

"She's just as intense as her dad," Spencer said. "It's the epitome of living on the edge. He took small vials of vamp blood from the office so no one noticed it missing." And Sierra gave him a space to use for coding, as well as the nightshade and wolfsbane in exchange for his silence. Quite the arrangement.

"And somehow the rest of you got roped in?" I queried.

Spencer got a faraway look in his eyes. "Jordy was so psyched about their first trip. She said it was like nothing she'd ever experienced. She begged her dad to let us try."

"And you all got hooked." It was more of a statement than a question.

"Big time."

"So the night Grover died, you pumped him full of nightshade and wolfsbane to bring him to death's door, but then ran out of vampire blood and couldn't revive him?"

"We used what was left of our stash, but it wasn't enough," Spencer said. "We'd all taken our turns that night. Grover was last." Spencer's gaze drifted to the floor. "We weren't in our right minds when we realized we couldn't bring him back. Someone started yelling about unicorn horns, so we all took off to find one."

"All except Bruce," I said.

"Yeah. Bruce stayed with Grover, but, by the time we came back, he was gone."

"Because he'd taken Grover to Balefire Beach."

Spencer pressed his fingers against the crystals. "Bruce had already been to see the sculptures. He knew if he buried him in the casket, he'd buy us time to work out our stories."

My thoughts turned to Cindy. "And who returned the phone to Grover's house? Was it you?"

He shook his head. "Jordy. Her dad was furious when he found out, but she said she wiped it clean."

"She did," I said. "But the gesture was enough to suggest that Grover's killer knew him and cared about him."

Spencer sniffed. "We did. Nobody meant for him to die. There's an insane amount of trust involved in coding. We brought each other close to death all the time, but we *always* brought each other back."

"Except the one time you didn't," I said.

Spencer's expression crumpled. "Yeah. I guess." He met my sorrowful gaze. "What will happen to us? Will we go to prison?"

"Not if I can help it," a rumbling voice said. A voice that made my skin crawl.

I clutched my wand and spun around. "What are you doing here, Bruce?"

"I had a talk with Sierra earlier tonight," Bruce said. "She mentioned running into you at the Whitethorn last night. That you and she were very chatty."

"What can I say? I'm easy to talk to."

"She may be a tough valkyrie, but she's not very smart," Bruce said.

"And you are?" I queried.

"Smart enough to put magical trackers on all the kids after the accident," Bruce said. "I had to be sure everyone stuck to the plan. Couldn't afford to have someone sneak off to the sheriff's office out of guilt."

"That's how you knew about Grover's phone, isn't it?" I asked. "You knew Jordy had been to Grover's house."

"I warned her to stay away from the family," Bruce said. "Let the dust settle. I don't like to be disobeyed." His nostrils flared as he looked at Spencer. "Go home, Spencer, and don't tell anyone you saw us here."

Spencer glanced wildly from Bruce to me. "What are you going to do?"

"Protect our interests, boy," Bruce growled. "What do you think? Now do as you're told."

Spencer ran from the room as fast as his satyr legs could carry him.

I took the momentary distraction as an opportunity to duck behind a row of gnomes. The room was dark enough that Bruce wouldn't easily spot me.

"There's no point in hiding. Come out and show yourself," he demanded. Based on his angry tone, that did not seem like a wise thing to do. I remained hidden behind the gnomes, weighing my options.

The centaur clip-clopped toward the ceramic army. "Come out now. You're going to lose, so you may as well stop wasting our time."

I was going to have to defend myself. My fingers gripped my wand. What kind of spell could I use on the powerful centaur? Whatever it was, I'd need to act quickly.

As I moved to extend my wand, my elbow knocked into one of the gnomes. I squeezed my eyes shut as the ceramic figure wobbled on the edge of the table. Thanks to my useless reflexes, I couldn't grab it in time. The gnome plunged to the floor and cracked. As the sound echoed through the room, Bruce halted in his tracks. A slow, menacing smile flattened his features and I shivered.

Think, Ember, I told myself. I could start chucking gnomes at him, but that would only slow him down, not stop him. An idea occurred to me. Would it work? Only one way to find out.

I focused my will, pointed my wand, and said, *"Anima."*

The garden gnome sprang to life. Gnomes alive—it worked! I aimed my wand again and again, invoking the same spell. The gnomes didn't hesitate to jump to my defense, leaping off the tables with gusto. They charged the centaur like they were in a *Lord of the Rings*-style battle. I couldn't decide whether Ian would be proud or horrified.

"You think you can defeat me with minions?" Bruce's booming laugh reverberated in the cavernous room. "Do you have any idea who I am? I was the colony champion. I'm a *winner.*"

The gnomes continued to charge him, grabbing his legs and launching themselves onto his back. They were vicious warriors. Eventually, it became clear that their valiant efforts wouldn't be enough to bring him down. I racked my brain for another spell—something that would subdue the powerful centaur.

Of course. The opposite spell! That would do the trick. Bruce was so intense and angry, that teasing out the opposite qualities could only help me.

I aimed my wand at the hulking centaur and fired. *"Contrarium."*

His massive body immediately relaxed and he regarded me with a mellow expression. "Hasn't there been enough violence? Maybe we can talk about this like two reasonable paranormals. Call off your totems. I'm sure we can come to an arrangement that satisfies us both."

The only arrangement that would satisfy me would be to see his hairy butt hauled off to prison. Still, I waved my wand like Ian did at the coven meeting, making an 'S' motion, and the gnomes returned to their lifeless ceramic forms.

"You killed Grover and permanently scarred three innocent kids," I said. "And for what?"

"Jordy's a champion, like her old man. She'll be just fine." He made a sailing motion with his hand.

"Let's see how much of a champion you are in prison, big guy." I retrieved my cell phone to call for help.

"Rose! Where are you?"

I couldn't believe my ears. "Sheriff?"

He appeared behind a trail of gnome carcasses, gaping at the unusual scene. "Great Goddess of the Moon! What happened in here?" He stooped to examine a pool of liquid on the floor. "Is that glue or blood?"

Please let it be glue.

"I'll explain later," I said, gesturing to the easygoing centaur. "First, get a pair of cuffs on this guy. How did you know I was here?" I patted myself down and prayed he didn't have a magical tracking device placed on me. I didn't need him to know exactly how many times I used the bathroom in a day. The size of my bladder was embarrassing.

"Spencer came to my house," he said. "Told me it was an emergency."

"Well done, Spencer," I whispered.

The sheriff shifted his focus to the centaur. "He didn't tell me the whole story, but he told me enough." The sheriff twirled a pair of large handcuffs in the air. "Bruce Hoskins, you're under arrest for the murder of Grover Maitland."

The centaur said nothing as he was hauled to his hooves.

"What about Sierra?" I asked. "She has a kiln full of illegal substances."

"I've already sent Deputy Bolan to her house with an arrest warrant," the sheriff said. "I'll take care of the building tomorrow."

"What about Jordy?" Bruce asked. "Will she lose her chance at a scholarship?"

"Let's focus on you for now," the sheriff said, and nudged the centaur toward the door. "You okay getting home, Rose, or do you want a ride?"

"I'm good. I need to clean up these gnomes. I made quite the mess."

He grinned. "Your specialty, isn't it? Anyway, it's a crime scene now. You need to leave it as is."

Right. "You go ahead and do your job," I told him. "I'll drive myself home. No need to worry about me."

He offered me a small smile. "I'll always worry about you, Rose. That's what happens when you care about somebody."

My throat tightened as the sheriff left with the guilty centaur in tow. Even after the night at Strange Brew with Alec, the sheriff still wanted me to know he cared. Talk about opposites.

I took one last look at the ceramic carnage before I went home. The only thing in the world I wanted to do right now was hug my daughter and thank the universe for keeping her safe.

CHAPTER 19

THE NEXT MORNING I grabbed a latte from the Caffeinated Cauldron and went straight to the office to type up my story and deal with a certain vampire I knew would be there alone at this hour.

A lump formed in my throat as I stood in the doorway of his office. The thought of reverting to our routine of suppression filled me with angst. Still, I knew it had to be done. I'd let the spell continue far longer than I should have and it was wrong. The moment I realized what had happened, I should've fixed it. The question was whether Alec would have any awareness of what had transpired or whether his memory would be wiped. I wasn't sure which I wanted more.

"Ember, what a wonderful surprise," he said, noticing my presence. "I'm so pleased to see you. How are you feeling? You left my place so abruptly the other night. I wasn't sure whether I'd done something to upset you."

"No, of course not," I said, and moved to sit in front of his desk so the furniture obscured his view.

"I heard about the arrests," he said. "I'm so glad you're

safe. You really ought to consider staying out of harm's way for a change."

"Yes, you're absolutely right." I retrieved my wand from my back pocket and focused my will, blinking back tears as I did so. I didn't realize the true extent of my feelings for him until this moment. I was letting him go and it hurt. I aimed the wand at his legs under the desk.

"You and the sheriff make an excellent team," he said. "I must admit to a bit of jealousy."

"*Novis*," I whispered. Why did doing the right thing feel so horribly wrong?

His green eyes glazed over as the magic left him. He blinked and glanced around the office before his gaze settled on me.

"Miss Rose?" he queried.

Miss Rose.

My heart plummeted. Alec Hale was back.

"What time is it?" he asked.

"Morning," I said. "Everything okay?"

He paused, considering the question. "I...think so. A story was relayed to me recently."

"A good one?"

"I'm not entirely certain. It was about an evening I spent with you." He immediately regretted his turn of phrase. "I mean, a dinner..." His expression slowly shifted as he appeared to remember the events of that evening. "We went to dinner, the two of us."

"We did. It was very nice. You told me your favorite dessert is crème brûlée and that you order it anytime you see it on a menu. You seemed very eager for me to know that." Tears stung my eyes as I remembered his delight in sharing such personal information. Alec—the vampire that refused to reveal his favorite type of coffee because he considered it an intimate detail—would be horrified when he remembered all that he'd shared with me that night.

"Crème brûlée," he repeated absently. "Yes, it was delicious."

"You said it was the best one you'd ever had." *And that I was the best kisser you'd ever had.* I made sure to cloak my thoughts so as not to trigger the memory.

"After dinner there was…" His brow furrowed. "No, I couldn't possibly have done…"

"Karaoke," I finished for him. Sheesh. He couldn't even say the word.

"Sheriff Nash was there. He and I participated in some sort of sing-off?" He seemed unclear about the details.

"You participated in more than that," I said vaguely. If he didn't mention our make-out session back at his place, then neither would I.

"And I won?" he queried.

I thought of the sheriff's sullen expression when I left with Alec. "You did, Alec. You won." And now we were both about to lose. I felt it in my bones and it sucked.

He went to adjust the knot of his tie before realizing he wasn't wearing one. "Miss Rose, I have no idea what possessed me to behave in such a manner. I simply would like to apologize if I misled you in any way."

Inwardly, I breathed a sigh of relief. So he didn't know it was my spell. As much as I wanted to, I couldn't bring myself to tell him the truth. I worried that he'd never speak to me again and I couldn't bear the thought of it.

"Misled me? Into thinking you were an amazing singer?" Which he was. Damn vampire and his endless talents.

His green eyes fixed on me. "Into thinking there can ever be more between us."

Ouch. That comment cut straight through my heart.

"You've been very clear about that, Alec. For what it's worth, we had a really nice time, and you were a natural performer."

"I have a vague recollection." He rubbed the back of his head. "It seems more like a dream."

To you and me both. "You showed me your manuscript. *Filthy Witch*."

He winced. "A temporary diversion, nothing more."

"I enjoyed the parts you read to me," I said. "I hope you publish it."

He looked deeply uncomfortable. "I should never have written it. I merely wanted to try my hand at a different kind of fantasy. Turns out it didn't suit me."

My chest began to ache. "I'm sorry to hear that."

"I understand the sheriff was quite put out after seeing us together," he said. "You should set him straight. He's one of the good ones, you know."

My eyebrows shot up. "Since when?"

He reached across the desk for me, but then quickly withdrew, thinking better of the gesture. "You deserve to be happy, Miss Rose. I have no business interfering with that."

I opened my mouth to speak, but no sound came out. I didn't know what to say. As much as I liked Sheriff Nash, I liked Alec, too. A lot. Sweet baby Twilight. When did life get so complicated?

"Don't feel like you need to apologize to me," I said. "You were a lot of fun. I'm sorry if the whole experience makes you uncomfortable. You don't ever need to feel that way with me, you know. I'm pretty laid-back."

"You have been...the easiest paranormal to talk to," he admitted. "And I enjoy your company immensely, but I promise you, it cannot lead to anywhere good."

I didn't want to argue with him. If his worldview was so skewed that a future with me was a foregone disaster, how on earth could I convince him otherwise?

"I wish you saw it differently," I said quietly.

"I'll have your story on Grover today, yes?"

Nausea rolled over me. This was it. Back to business as usual. "Yes, of course," I said.

"Anything I can help with?"

"No, I can handle it on my own." Why should Starry Hollow be any different from New Jersey?

"Of course you can. Good day, Miss Rose."

"See you around, Alec." I'd have to finish Grover's story at the cottage. There was no way I could stay in the office with him right now. I hurried from the building before my cloaking abilities collapsed under the strain of emotional weight. I didn't want him to know how deeply he'd hurt me. I deserved it, after all. If my punishment was to suffer in guilty silence, then so be it.

Florian took center stage, practically vibrating with powerful energy. It was no surprise he was a celebrity in Starry Hollow.

"Thank you all for coming today," he said. There was no microphone required. A little magic amplified the sound so the entire assembled crowd could hear his smooth voice. "Welcome to the first annual Starry Hollow sand sculpture competition."

Applause erupted, along with wolf whistles and cheers. I spotted Wyatt in the crowd, murmuring in a young nymph's ear. I'd managed to quietly reverse the spell on him without anyone noticing. I still felt guilty over the whole incident. It was only meant to be a joke on Hazel and I took it too far. Lesson learned. Even though Opposite Wyatt was preferable to Actual Wyatt in everyone's book, it didn't matter. Any real change had to come from Wyatt himself.

"As I'm sure you're aware, the town suffered a great loss

recently," Florian continued. "We'd like to dedicate the competition to the memory of Grover Maitland."

Heads turned toward Grover's parents standing with Cindy at the bottom of the stage.

"I'd also like to announce that the Rose Foundation is establishing a Grover Maitland Memorial Fund to support non-athletic extracurricular activities for local high school students."

It had been an easy decision for the family. Even Aunt Hyacinth voted in favor of the fund, and I thought for sure she'd be the lone voice of dissent.

"Now, the moment you've all been waiting for," Florian said. "We're pleased to announce the top three winners for their incredible craftsmanship. Third place goes to Thomas Enders."

I clapped loudly for the vampire undertaker. Thomas appeared onstage with a ninja-like quality I usually attributed to my vampire boss. My gut twisted at the thought of Alec. I knew he wasn't here today. Tanya said he'd taken an unexpected trip out of town and she didn't know when he'd return. I blamed myself, of course. He'd been fine in his comfort zone, and I'd ruined it with my stupid spell.

"Thomas receives a year's supply of ice cream from Stars and Cones," Florian announced. "Thanks to the owners for supporting the tourism board and this competition."

Thomas gave an awkward wave to the crowd before accepting his certificate.

"Second place is awarded to Adam Forrest for the maze sculpture," Florian said.

Marley jumped up and down. "That was such a good one."

Adam shuffled up to accept his award and I noticed Rick in the crowd. It was difficult not to. He waved when he saw me.

"Who's that?" Marley asked, distracted by the enormous minotaur.

"His name is Rick. He and Adam co-own Paradise Found, the garden center."

Marley continued to stare. "His horns are huge. How does he get in and out of doorways?"

"He has his tricks," I said.

"Does he now?" Linnea asked, peering around me to glimpse the minotaur.

"I'll introduce you later," I said. "I think you'd really like him."

"I wouldn't object to finding out," my cousin replied.

Florian announced that the sorcerer's prize was a trip for two to Castaway Cove. I didn't miss the hopeful expression on Adam's face as he located Rick in the crowd. Rick, of course, was too busy looking in our direction to notice. I felt a pang of sympathy for the kind sorcerer. Unrequited feelings were the worst.

"I think we can all agree on the first place winner," Florian said. "Maisie Cranshaw, please come up and accept your prize. A very generous gift card for The Magic Words."

"The castle," Marley cried, delighted.

"There was no contest, really," I said. The pixie's attention to detail was unrivaled.

Maisie seemed nervous to accept her award from Florian. Her wings fluttered so fast, they were almost invisible.

"Would you like to say a few words?" he prompted.

Maisie glanced at the crowd. "I'm used to addressing teenagers and their parents in a school setting. This crowd is a tad bit bigger." She cleared her throat. "Thank you for this award. I'm proud of my work, but I'd like to take a moment to talk about Grover Maitland." She made brief eye contact with the Maitland family before she continued. "He was a lovely elf with a ready smile and an inquisitive mind. He liked the stories in history class, but he hated memorizing facts. Although he pretended to be annoyed by her, he loved his little sister fiercely. He even mentioned her in class on occasion because she was the one who shared stories with him about the historical figures in our textbook. He pretended not to be interested, I'm sure." She smiled at the young elf. "But he was listening, Cindy. Trust me, he was."

The Maitlands huddled together, as though a strong gust of wind might blow them apart.

Maisie finished her speech and shook Florian's hand again before blending with the bodies on the beach.

I didn't waste any time introducing Linnea to Rick. He seemed to take her blinding beauty in stride. Linnea needed someone who wouldn't be intimidated by her or her famous family. Or her ex-husband, for that matter. I had a feeling Rick would be an ideal choice.

And now it was my daughter's turn for companionship.

"Come on, Marley," I said, taking her by the hand. "There's a little girl called Cindy I want you to meet."

Once Marley and Cindy discovered their mutual love of books, it was clear I was no longer needed. Marley shooed me away and I took full advantage, intending to have another look at the winning sandcastle. As I ventured inside for another tour, Sheriff Nash slipped in behind me.

"There you are, Rose," he said. "Been looking all over for you."

I continued working my way through the castle, admiring the details I'd missed the last time. "Not very hard," I replied. "I was right in front of the stage."

"With Hale?" he asked. I detected a hard edge to the question.

"No, Alec's gone out of town," I said. "I don't know when he'll be back."

The sheriff moved to stand beside me as I appreciated the

large sand-sculpted fireplace. "Don't know when he'll be back, huh? I thought you two were declaring your eternal love for each other." He paused. "That's the way it seemed at Strange Brew, anyway."

"You should know better than that," I said. "First of all, there's no such thing as eternal love."

The sheriff frowned. "That's a bit cynical, Rose, even for you."

I experienced an unexpected rush of anger. I knew it was misplaced, but I couldn't stop myself.

"I never asked for any of this, you know," I said, waving my arms around like a lunatic. "Marley and I were fine back in New Jersey. Okay, my life may not have been perfect, but at least it wasn't painful. We had the basics down—heat in the winter, food, and electricity. Marley was excelling, of course, because she's amazing. She's like the tree that grows in Brooklyn."

The sheriff cocked his head. "What tree?"

"Never mind," I said heatedly. "The point is—I didn't ask for this life. I could've continued down the path of ignorance and Marley and I would have been absolutely fine." A simple life with PP3 in our two-bedroom apartment, uncomplicated by strong emotions and family ties.

"But wouldn't you rather be better than fine?" the sheriff asked softly.

I fell silent. Alec was right; Sheriff Nash was a good guy. He didn't deserve my frustration. It should've been Alec standing here, enduring my freak-out moment.

The sheriff took a step closer. "Listen, Rose. I don't know exactly what happened between you and Hale. Frankly, I prefer it that way. The fact remains that, for whatever strange reason, I have these pesky feelings for you that refuse to go away." He let his words sink in. "So, if you're interested in being better than fine, I'd like to roll the runes and see where this relationship goes."

Relationship? The word made me shudder. "I don't know, Sheriff. You've got to feel like I'm not worth the trouble at this point."

He placed both hands on my shoulders and looked me squarely in the eye. "For starters, I'd like you to call me Granger. And you're right, Rose. You're a heap of trouble, but I think you're worth it." He gave me a lopsided grin. "And, let's face it, sometimes trouble can be fun."

"You think I'm fun?" I echoed. "Not a pain in the butt? The intrepid witch that interferes with your ability to do your job?"

"You're all those things, Rose, but they're not deal break-ers. I still want to spend time with you. Get to know you more." He stopped talking and scratched his scruffy jaw. "Do you want me to stop calling you Rose? I feel like a hypocrite telling you to call me Granger and I'm still using your last name."

I couldn't resist a smile. "Honestly? I don't mind when you call me Rose."

"Good." He cocked his head. "You *are* interested, aren't you? I'm not making up this thing between us in my dim werewolf brain."

"Your brain isn't dim, Granger," I said, and his name felt odd on my tongue. "It isn't that I'm not interested. It's just that I've been confused and...overwhelmed by so much change. I haven't been in a relationship since Karl—haven't even looked—and in Starry Hollow I've been..." I struggled to find the right words. Words that captured my asylum-worthy state of mind. Finally, I let out an exasperated sigh. "My life feels very complicated."

His brow wrinkled. "So what does that mean? You don't want to date at all?"

"It means I want to take it slowly," I said. I'd jumped into Alec's arms at the first opportunity and look where that stupidity got me. I wasn't going to make the same mistake with the sheriff.

He looped his fingers through mine. "You set the pace, Rose. Watching you that night at karaoke..." He shook his head, remembering. "I realized I wasn't doing myself any favors by holding back and acting cool. I hated seeing you with Hale. Life's too short for regrets, but if you need to move slowly, then I understand."

I stared at the sheriff—at Granger. He was absolutely right. Life *was* too short. My parents had taught me that. Karl had taught me that, too. When would I learn the lesson the universe was desperate to teach me?

"What? No snappy comeback?" the sheriff prodded.

His hand was warm over mine. I stared at his fingers, strong and reassuring. In that brief moment, I understood what Linnea must have seen in Wyatt all those years ago. Why she threw caution to the wind, despite her mother's objections.

"Why don't you come over for dinner next weekend?" I asked. "Saturday."

"To the cottage?" he asked, surprised.

"Yes, I'll cook for you and Marley." And hoped no one suffered horribly as a result.

He appeared pleased. "Are you sure? It's a big deal, right? Having someone over to spend time with your daughter?"

I nodded. "It is a big deal, Granger. The question is—are you up for it?"

He puffed out his chest so that his gold star gleamed in the sunlight. "For you, Rose? Always."

* * *

If you want to find out about new releases by Annabel Chase, sign up for my newsletter here: http://eepurl.com/ctYNzf

Starry Hollow Witches

Magic & Murder, Book 1

Magic & Mystery, Book 2

Magic & Mischief, Book 3

Magic & Mayhem, Book 4

Magic & Mercy, Book 5

Magic & Madness, Book 6

Spellbound

Curse the Day, Book 1

Doom and Broom, Book 2

Spell's Bells, Book 3

Lucky Charm, Book 4

Better Than Hex, Book 5

Cast Away, Book 6

A Touch of Magic, Book 7

A Drop in the Potion, Book 8

Hemlocked and Loaded, Book 9

All Spell Breaks Loose, Book 10